When she retraced her steps back to him, Nasser had to forcibly unclench his jaw to grit out, "You are safe with me."

Anisa sniffed. "You say that, but I don't know you—"

He closed the gap between them, and she cut herself off and took one sharp inhale in reaction.

"I repeat—your safety is paramount to me. Do not take my words lightly either."

With her hijab styled as a turban, he could see her throat ripple in response to his words. Backdropped by the purple blooms of the jacaranda, Anisa made for a mesmerizing portrait. It was one he unconsciously cataloged for memory as his stare roved over the rosy-brown flush painting the tip of her nose and the swell of her cheeks. The longer he studied her, the louder her breathing became in the silence, her lips parting. Fighting not to close his eyes, he subtly pulled in her natural scent. But how could anyone smell so good? Feeling the same kind of breathlessness, he stepped to the side, discreetly giving them the space they both seemed to need.

As soon as he did, Anisa's lips tightened and her nostrils flared, but she didn't argue.

T0197846

Dear Reader,

There's nothing more gratifying in a romance to me than following an emotionally wounded character's journey of personal healing to a happily-ever-after.

In *Falling for Her Forbidden Bodyguard*, Anisa and Nasser are at odds with each other. Nasser just wants to do the job Anisa's brother hired him for and safeguard Anisa, but she wants her independence and doesn't want to be babysat by a bodyguard (no matter how hot he is!). On top of this, they are both deeply impacted by childhood losses. So much, in fact, that they can't recognize the power of trusting and leaning on loved ones when they are at their lowest points.

Because of this distrust, they keep their hearts closely guarded. It takes a journey together across the paradise-like island of Madagascar all the way to the shores of Somalia for them to realize they not only share a lot in common, but that they can help one another heal from and grow through their individual traumas.

So if you're anything like me and love a tale where good people are hurting *and* get their happy at the end, then I hope Anisa and Nasser's love story satisfies you.

Happy reading,

Hana

FALLING FOR HER FORBIDDEN BODYGUARD

HANA SHEIK

ROMANCE

Harlequin®
ROMANCE

ISBN-13: 978-1-335-21607-6

Falling for Her Forbidden Bodyguard

Copyright © 2024 by Muna Sheik

Recycling programs for this product may not exist in your area.

Harlequin Enterprises ULC
22 Adelaide St. West, 41st Floor
Toronto, Ontario M5H 4E3, Canada
www.Harlequin.com

Printed in U.S.A.

Hana Sheik falls in love every day reading her favorite romances and writing her own happily-ever-afters. She's worked various jobs—but never for very long because she's always wanted to be a romance author. Now she gets to happily live that dream. Born in Somalia, she moved to Ottawa, Canada, at a very young age and still resides there with her family.

Books by Hana Sheik

Harlequin Romance

Second Chance to Wear His Ring
Temptation in Istanbul
Forbidden Kisses with Her Millionaire Boss
The Baby Swap That Bound Them

Visit the Author Profile page at Harlequin.com.

To Soraya,
For taking the messy first draft of this story, seeing
what it could become and making it sparkle.

**Praise for
Hana Sheik**

"*Second Chance to Wear His Ring* is so much
more than a typical romance story. It is a story of
overcoming personal tragedy and also has
huge cultural references!"

—*Goodreads*

CHAPTER ONE

Take care of yourself.

ANISA ABDULLAHI READ the text from her older brother, Ara, as she had several times throughout her long flight from Canada to Madagascar, yet it still elicited the same shock from her.

A shock she had every right to feel.

Ara hadn't spoken to her in four years, cutting off all communication when Anisa had decided to leave their family home in Berbera, Somaliland, to pursue an education and a career in Toronto. It was petty of him, but he'd wanted her to know that he was displeased with her choice. At first Anisa had met his cold shoulder with her own childish behavior. Blocking him on all social media had been a way to push him out of her life. She knew that nothing would aggravate him more than not being able to immediately access what she was up to. After all, Ara had shunned her in the first place because he had lost his precious control over her.

A control he'd exerted to protect her…or so he would have her believe. Anisa only went along with his obsessive helicoptering for the sake of their long-dead parents. She'd told herself so many times that Ara *needed* to do what he had to do to save the family he had left: her. Losing their mother and father had changed him, and it took her a long while to realize that his change wasn't for the better.

And that was why she refused to be the one to break their silence.

At least, that was how she felt. Over time, Anisa's embittered heart stirred with a longing. For family. For her brother. Not the man who imprisoned her in their home and tracked her every innocent movement with eagle-eyed precision. Rather, the boy who after pranking her would laugh so hard he'd get a bellyache, but who would then just as easily chase off her school bullies.

She wanted that version of her brother.

Almost as much as she'd just wished for some sign, *any* sign that he wasn't gravely upset with her anymore.

Though admittedly the long-awaited message from Ara wasn't exactly as she'd pictured.

"'Take care of yourself'… What does that even mean, and how am I supposed to reply back?" she muttered under her breath before dropping her phone in her lap and massaging her throbbing temples. Her hands stilled suddenly when she considered that maybe Ara had messaged her accidentally.

He meant to text someone else, not me.

She sighed, supposing that the universe was having some good fun at her expense.

She'd only waited for most of four insufferably long years to hear from her brother—

"And now I need cipher to decode his message. Great." Anisa groaned, biting back her sarcastic moaning halfway when two businessmen sitting in chairs nearest to her stopped chatting and eyed her funnily.

With a blush, and a softer groan of embarrassment, Anisa sank into the comfortable armchair in the hotel's foyer. Before she could hope to disappear, she caught the eyes of another person.

A man standing before the revolving glass doors of the hotel's entrance and exit.

Anisa's breath whooshed out, not remembering when she held in the gulp of air. She must have, after noticing the handsome stranger who seemed to be watching her. He was dressed in business attire like the men who had looked at her strangely, but unlike them, his suit molded seamlessly to unmistakable muscle, hinting at the exquisite work of a tailor handling expensive material for his creation. The result was a jacket and pants of obsidian, with a pale gray dress shirt and a gleaming white tie. He was a monochromatic emblem. One that had her discreetly wiping at her mouth after picking her jaw up off the floor.

In fairness, it was the only appropriate reaction to a man who looked that good.

A man who really, truly *did* appear to be boring holes into her skull from the short distance that separated them.

Instinctively Anisa slid up the chair, sitting straighter, with her hands fastening on the supple leather of the armrests and her sneakers pressed flat to the soft rug carpeting the waiting area. She looked around, certain there was a perfectly logical explanation.

Someone's standing behind me, that's it. Probably a gorgeous bikini-clad woman heading toward the hotel's crystal-blue outdoor pool.

Only she had seen the sign pointing to the pool, and it was in the opposite direction from the foyer, nearer the back of the hotel for privacy.

Yet because it was far more plausible to believe than thinking this hot dude was checking her out, she clung to the woman-in-a-bikini theory.

But no one conveniently stood behind her to explain who he'd been looking at. No half-dressed woman sauntered along the foyer. There was no one but her. And that unleashed a torrent of heat through her blood, her skin flushing readily, her limbs weakening just as her heart strengthened its beats. It wasn't an entirely awful feeling. Strange, unexpected…

Not terrible, icky, or ugly and unwanted.

But she suddenly experienced a vulnerability she wanted to outrun. That explained her physical reaction.

She wanted to get out of there.

When she tried to move, get up from the chair and rush back to the sanctuary of her hotel room, Anisa couldn't budge. Couldn't bring herself to do anything but gawk at the devastatingly handsome man staring her down from across the brightly lit foyer.

So Anisa studied his heart-stopping features. And she missed nothing, her eyes tracking almost hungrily over his short, curly black hair and the low fade that started right around his ears. From there her gaze traveled over his big shoulders, his strong, distinct jawline, up to his well-cut cheekbones, broad-tipped nose, and thick black eyebrows that lowered subtly now that she was noticing. His lushly round lips, dusky in color, curled with the beginnings of a frown under her observation.

But it was his eyes that arrested her mind completely. Fathomlessly dark pupils beheld her as though no one else existed…despite there being several people in the entrance hall with them.

I'm imagining things. Any minute now he's going to raise his hand, and somebody else will pop up. Any moment he'll look away. Any second—

If Anisa held another thought in her head, it

flew away the instant he suddenly moved in her direction, and along with it any hope to sneak off.

She froze, a doe trapped in a hunter's snare.

In college she'd worked as a paid student assistant on a nature documentary at a Florida wild cat sanctuary. Right now she was having flashbacks of the big cats she had met. Specifically the rare black panther. Only this man wasn't prowling toward her on all fours. Rather, his steps were unhurried in polished brown cap-toe oxfords. And it seemed to her that, like an apex predator's, his stare intensified upon approach.

Another few strides and he'd be right by her side.

What am I going to say?

Anisa's heart rate quickened as her mind flailed. The worst part was she knew that she wouldn't be able to utter the first word, not with the way her jaw slackened and her tongue grew stiff in her mouth.

It didn't stop her from trying. She pried her drying lips apart—

"Anisa! There you are!"

Anisa jerked her head to see her coworker and friend Darya hurrying toward her from the elevator. She blinked in surprise, once, twice, before finally shaking off the stupor clouding her head and discovering she could move her limbs again.

She stood as Darya touched her arm, concern painting her friend's pale, round face.

"I've been calling you," Darya said. "Weren't we supposed to meet up in your room first before heading out?"

Because they'd only landed a couple hours ago, and it was well into the evening in Madagascar's capital, Antananarivo, their film crew wouldn't officially begin work until tomorrow morning. Once production started, there was very little chance they would have time to themselves outside the long hours that awaited them, especially as they had one day allotted in Antananarivo for their filming schedule. That meant she and Darya had the best chance to do a little city exploring tonight and tonight only.

"Sorry, I got bored and decided to come down for a little people-watching." Anisa cast her friend a sheepish smile.

"Well, if you're done scoping out the other hotel guests, may we please go catch our rideshare before it decides to leave us?" Darya batted her long fake lashes for comical effect.

Anisa snorted a laugh.

Darya grinned before hooking her arm through Anisa's and pulling her toward the exit.

Anisa's humor dried up on recalling that there was one hotel guest in particular who had consumed most of her attention. She spotted him at Reception, speaking to the staff behind the large circular bronze and white marble desk. Looking back to the armchair she'd vacated, she figured it was possible that he'd been aiming for the hotel's front desk all along, and that she'd let her imagination get the better of her.

There was no way he was coming for me.

The thought carried some relief and a smidgen of dismay.

Even when she'd wanted to run, she wouldn't have minded a guy *that* incredibly hot focusing all his attention on her.

Allowing Darya to tug her through the revolving doors out into the city, Anisa flung a final look back at him before losing sight of him altogether, then forced herself to release her strange bout of disappointment.

Surely there were other attractive men in the world. Maybe even some who were actually interested in her.

So why couldn't she get this one out of her head?

Anisa couldn't figure out if she was losing her mind or not. But she didn't know how else she could explain seeing her stranger from the hotel all over the Analakely Market, a popular outdoor marketplace in Antananarivo, or Tana, as the locals called the city. At first, it was just glimpses from the corner of her eye.

In the narrow paths snaking between vendor stalls. Behind her in the sea of bodies flooding the market space.

He seemed to be everywhere—and nowhere at the same time.

Even when she paused to right her hijab, using her phone's camera as an impromptu mirror, her hands froze at the sight of those dark eyes searing her. Yet when Anisa whirled around…no one was there.

But when she saw him striding past the large front window of the small restaurant she and Darya had chosen to dine at, Anisa began to question her sanity.

He can't be stalking me…

Anisa wished her confidence backed her thinking. She continued to feel out of sorts after she and Darya split their dinner bill and left the restaurant, strolling back through the expansive market.

Spread over several blocks, Analakely Market had almost everything, from produce, seafood and meat to clothing, shoes, household items and bootleg films. In that way, it was not unlike most outdoor marketplaces. But it also had unique perks like pop-up nail salons served solely by young men, and grilled lizard meat among other traditional street foods.

Anisa sniffed the air laced with the tantalizing smells, though luckily her stomach was immune to the scents. The big Malagasy-style dinner she'd shared with Darya had saved her from shelling out more money sampling the foods from the market vendors.

Walking past the delectable, deep-fried temptations on display, Anisa trailed her friend to a stall selling hats of all kinds.

The stall owner, an elderly woman with brown skin lined with age, smiled widely in recognition of them. Like most of the market vendors, she was eager to make a sale. Happy to oblige, Darya zeroed in on a fedora.

She popped the hat on and modeled it for Anisa. "Does it make my head look big?"

Anisa disagreed with a laugh.

Smiling her approval, Darya started haggling over the price with the stall owner.

Free to look around the nearby stalls, Anisa paused at a table full of sparkly trinkets, never thinking she would see so many hair clips and ties, ribbons, and bedazzled broaches all in one place. She was looming over the rhinestone-embellished silver pins when the vendor encouraged her to try some on. Eagerly Anisa clipped a bow-shaped pin to her hijab and studied her reflection in the hand mirror the vendor offered her.

Even with the small cracks in the smudged mirror, she couldn't deny the attractiveness of the accessory.

Parting with a few Malagasy ariary, the local currency, wasn't an issue.

As she strolled away with her new purchase

pinned to her hijab, Anisa hoped Darya was done with her price negotiation so that they could finally leave the market and head for their hotel.

Between Ara's enigmatic text and believing that she had a handsome stalker, her day could be summed up as a wild roller-coaster ride, and she couldn't wait for it to end. Pulling her phone up by its long, pearly cross-body chain, Anisa scrolled past Ara's message and thumbed a quick text for Darya to meet up with her at one of the three long stone stairways that led in and out of the market. Her thighs and calves already burned in anticipation of the workout she'd be getting from climbing all those steps up to La Ville Moyenne, the city's Middle Town, where they could hail a cab easier. She wasn't looking forward to it, yet if it meant that she could lock herself in her hotel suite and pretend she had no worries, then Anisa was up for the exercise.

After she sent Darya the message, she bobbed and weaved through the crowds back to where she'd left her friend and wondered how she'd managed to wander away so far, then came to an abrupt halt.

Anisa did a double take, gawking ahead of her, the crowds milling around blocking her view. Springing up on her toes, she searched avidly for some sort of confirmation this time.

Because she saw him again. The stranger from the hotel.

Only just as before, when she searched hard for him, he vanished. No trace or indication that he'd ever been there.

A tug on her shirt from behind startled her. Anisa whirled on a young boy in an old, faded shirt and shorts, his oversized and overly worn sandals caked with grime and dust. He looked up at her with large, dark eyes, held out both hands and said something pleadingly in French.

Anisa didn't need a translation app to understand what he was asking for. She rooted for some change and passed it to him. No sooner than she did, more children and even some adults approached her with outstretched hands. She didn't have spare change for them all and knew that she would have to back out of the situation she'd created. But they circled her, and she saw no direct path to slip away.

They crowded closer.

Someone stepped on her foot, an elbow dug into her side, and her phone chain was yanked roughly from behind.

If claustrophobia wasn't an issue before, she feared it would be after this.

"I don't have any more money. I'm sorry— *désolée*," she pleaded, barely recalling how to say *sorry* in French. True fear pricked her heart when the beggars, not heeding her plea, pushed in closer, crowding her personal space.

Not knowing what else to do, Anisa kept backing away helplessly. Right into a solid wall...of unyieldingly hard and very warm muscle.

She lurched forward away from the person she'd bumped into and turned to face them with a ready apology.

An apology that never fully formed as her jaw dropped open.

"It's you!"

Those *weren't* the words she'd pictured coming from her, but they seemed appropriate enough when she came face to face with the stranger from the hotel.

Just as appropriately, she followed that surprised observation with, "Are you stalking me?"

Of all the terrible things Nasser Dirir had been called—a rebel, a criminal, a heartless monster—he'd never expected to add *stalker* to the list.

"Well, are you? Stalking me?" Hurling the query at him, Anisa shuffled away, just as she had when the beggars flocked to her. As though he posed a real threat.

Her defensive posture shouldn't have bothered him, but it did, and somehow that irked him even more than her downright rude accusation.

It took everything in him to rise above his steaming annoyance and ignore her question. He skipped to the part where he dangled her phone in front of her face, clutching it by its gaudily bejeweled chain. Of course he had to hold the ends of the now broken chain together or else risk the phone dropping and possibly breaking.

"This is yours, is it not?"

Anisa shifted her narrowed gaze from him to the phone swinging between them. He raised it higher so there would be no doubt who it belonged to. Her eyes widened with recognition, the light of a nearby lamppost reflecting off the dark of her irises.

And before she could open that mouth and sting him with her tongue again, he explained, "You should be careful. This pretty string might as well be a sparkling target for pickpockets." He emphasized his point when the streetlight glinted off the milky-white pearls on the phone chain.

She grabbed at the phone, and Nasser let her have it without a fight.

After checking it over, she looked up at him, her accusatory glare gone. "I didn't think someone stole my phone."

"They didn't get far."

"You caught them," she breathed, looking behind him, as though he had the petty thief in cuffs.

"Yes, and then I let the child go."

"Child?"

"A boy. No more than ten. It was enough that he was scared. I didn't see a need to drag him before the *gendarmerie*." That and the local police would only further traumatize the child thief.

Nasser clenched his jaw, leaving out the part that would reveal his…unresolved issues with police officials and other authority figures.

He hadn't realized he'd been holding a breath until Anisa nodded, silently agreeing with his decision to let her pickpocket go free.

"Well, thank you for recovering my phone." She pursed her lips, her body language shifting again, and he should've seen what was coming. "Though that doesn't explain why you followed me from the hotel."

So much for getting through to her.

Allah give me strength.

How was it that she still believed him to be a stalker? Nasser curbed a frustrated growl that managed to roll like ominous thunder through his gritted teeth. "Your brother sent me."

Anisa blinked, her face an open book conveying her shock.

"He didn't tell you," Nasser commented briskly, knowing it to be true and not needing her to confirm it. Her expression was answer enough. Barely containing his irritation, he said, "Ara hired me to watch over you, and he gave me the impression that he'd be informing you of that fact." The contract was signed and sealed, the price of his hire paid in full and nonrefundable.

"What do you mean, he sent you to watch over me?" Anisa asked.

"He feels you could benefit from some protection."

"Protection."

She said the word slowly as if to let its meaning sink in. Then she shook her head, muttering so quietly he almost missed what she said. "So that's why he messaged." He detected a flicker of sadness.

"Anisa? Anisa!"

Nasser watched the petite, pale-haired, pale-faced woman who had been with Anisa since the hotel break through the market crowds and come to a breathless stop beside her. If it hadn't been for her friend's interference, Nasser would've approached Anisa in the hotel lobby and introduced himself far earlier, sparing them both from the embarrassing debacle of having Anisa believe him to be a stalker.

"I got your message, but when I tried calling, you didn't pick up." Her friend trailed off, pushing up the fedora on her head before flicking a glance at him. "Who's he?"

Anisa looked over at him, the frown unbudging on her face.

"No one," she said quickly. Taking her friend's arm, she pulled her along, away from him and toward the steep stairway that marked the market's entrance and exit.

She might believe she'd shaken him off, but Nasser knew better.

He would see her again. Tomorrow, in fact, and the day after, and the day after that, because her brother had paid him handsomely to do his job.

And unfortunately for her, she *happens to be that job.*

CHAPTER TWO

"OKAY, SO YOUR brother sent a hot bodyguard—and why are we angry about that?"

Anisa huffed humorlessly and rolled her eyes at Darya's comment. It was simple for her friend to jest and make light of the situation, but she wasn't standing in her shoes, feeling betrayed. Her brother had gone behind her back and sent a stranger to shadow her. Ara didn't have to say he didn't trust her; his actions spoke for him clearly. His distrust of her was why Anisa had ultimately chosen to leave his side and chance being frozen out of his life.

Does he really believe that I can't take care of myself?

Sadly, she knew the answer to that question. But what cut the deepest and stung the most was that Ara had finally messaged her *only* out of some clear need to step in as her overprotective older brother once more.

I let him get to me...

She had herself to blame, yet it didn't mean that

her hands were tied. Anisa didn't have to suffer a bodyguard, attractive or otherwise.

"I'm going to tell him I don't want a bodyguard," Anisa said. The idea had come to her after she'd tossed and turned and pounded her pillow one too many times last night. It was the most sensible thing to do. And since she had no need of a bodyguard, surely her stranger from the hotel wouldn't force the matter. "He'll probably be relieved that he doesn't have to do his tedious job."

Her searching gaze landed on her unwanted bodyguard standing poised under the shade of a large tree several meters from her.

They were filming on the grounds of the Rova of Antananarivo, a royal palace complex atop the second tallest hills in the capital city. Formerly the seat of major political decisions and a home to the Merina monarchs who once ruled the southeast African island nation, in modern times the Rova was a tourist attraction. The film crew had set up in the front yard of the Queen's Palace, one of a dozen structures that remained standing in the former royal complex.

An impressive building, the palace had been gutted by a fire decades ago. It awaited completion of restoration work to regain its glory.

Scaffolding from the ongoing renovation wrapped the building, and tarps hanging in some of the palace's windows flapped in the easy wind. Anisa saw beyond the construction equipment to the palace's architectural beauty and the riches of its history. But with the day still so early, and the yard outside the palace looking so empty, its grandeur wouldn't be admired by anyone else right then except her fellow crewmates.

And though emptier for the lack of tourists, the buzz of activity in the yard was still loud. Soon they would begin filming, and Anisa would miss her window of opportunity to dismiss her brother's hired man.

She set aside the gaffer tape she was using to connect set equipment wires and marched for her target.

He didn't step out from the tree's dappled shade on her approach. Anisa stopped in front of him, her head tilting back and compensating for their significant height difference. But she didn't need an extra six or so inches to make herself feel taller. Her confidence came from her unflappable determination to get him to leave her alone.

"I'm not sure exactly what my brother has said to you, but I'm not in need of protection of any sort." She jutted her chin higher to punctuate her point.

His lips appeared to hike on one side, until she blinked and any evidence of a smile vanished.

"I'm sure my brother paid you already."

"*Oui*. He did, and quite generously," he confirmed, his voice as meltingly smooth as his French.

He was wearing business attire again, minus

his suit jacket this time. The slate-gray suit vest and dark gray tie popped against the pristine white of his button-down shirt, whose sleeves he'd rolled up. He had his legs crossed at the ankles, a shoulder pressed to the tree, and his arms crossed over his chest. Designer aviator sunglasses obfuscated his eyes, yet she couldn't deny feeling the weight of his stare.

"Great!" She clapped her hands together and forced a smile. "Then you can take that advance payment and leave me."

Anisa basked in the glow of her good idea, anticipating that he'd be glad to be rid of the duty imposed on him by her brother. But the longer she waited for his agreement, the more aware she became that it wasn't coming.

"If you're worried I'll say something to my brother, don't be." It wasn't like she was close to Ara anymore, and she doubted he told a random bodyguard he hired all about his strained relationship with his sister. "He doesn't need to know, and you can let him believe you performed your job."

He was still unmoved. His shoulder remained leaning on the broad tree trunk.

She quieted the urge to fidget from frustration. What did she have to say to get a reaction from him?

To get him to go away!

"I don't even know your name," Anisa blurted, not sure why she was so curious suddenly.

"Nasser," he said, his accent rolling the end of his name. "Being on a first-name basis isn't of import though."

Anisa put her hands on her hips. "Let me guess. My safety's more important."

"It matters to your brother."

"And because he hired you, it's now your concern too." She shifted her glare off to the side, where the production crew was wrapping up. Soon the assistant director would be calling both crew and cast to their posts for filming. Any time she had left for persuading Nasser to abandon his guard duty was coming to a fast close.

Biting her lip to prevent herself from letting out a shout of frustration, she presented a calm front she wasn't feeling at all.

"Fine. Then tell me *why* my brother's hired you now. Why suddenly send protection?"

"Isn't that a question better posed to your brother?"

Anisa breathed sharply through her nose, feeling her nostrils flare with her indignation.

It was a mistake she regretted the instant her lungs were saturated with the scent of him. A blend of freshest mint and earthy notes she couldn't quite name, Nasser's cologne swarmed into her twitching nose on the balmy October morning breeze. She fought against closing her eyes and inhaling him unabashedly.

Nasser looked just as enticing as he smelled.

Golden streams of dawn sunlight dappled his deep, rich brown skin.

Before she got too swept up in his attractive physical qualities, she realized just how physically close they were.

When did that happen?

Though startled, Anisa rectified that immediately. Once she established a polite distance between them, she retrained her glare on him, reminding herself that he wasn't there to be ogled. That as he ignored her demands, he was quickly making himself her enemy.

With that firmly in mind, she tried reasoning with him again, mindful of breathing in any more of his aromatic scent. "If you're not going to leave, the least you could do is tell me what he's up to that requires my protection. You both owe me that much if you insist on disrupting my life."

"It's not my place to speak for your brother. I insist you direct your inquiries to him."

I can't! Because then I'd have to talk to Ara, and I won't give him that satisfaction—not now, not after this, she wanted to holler.

Behind her, she heard the call from the assistant director for crew members to get into their places for filming to commence.

She was out of time.

She could see it from the way Nasser looked at her, his immovable expression and relaxed posture reading almost smug to her.

Annoyed beyond comprehension, and also too flustered for comfort, Anisa huffed and whirled away from Nasser, storming back to where she had been working before drifting over to chat with him.

Not long after, Darya appeared at her side.

"Is he leaving?" her friend asked.

Anisa glowered at Nasser watching her and grumbled, "No, and it was like getting a great big lump of a stone to budge. I might as well have been talking to a wall."

"You're going to have to tell the director about your bodyguard hanging around."

Anisa glared harder at Nasser, not happy that she had to report her personal affairs to her boss. "I'll tell him."

"Why not just text your brother and let him know how you feel?"

"At first, I wanted to. I just didn't know how to reply to his message. Then I started telling myself that maybe he'd accidentally messaged me when he meant to actually text someone else." She gave Darya a tight smile. "And now, after this bodyguard stuff, I don't want to give him the satisfaction of messaging."

"Are you giving up, then?" Darya wondered.

"No," she said resolutely. Her words might not have gotten through to Nasser, but her defeat only motivated her that much more.

One way or another, Anisa would make him leave.

* * *

Nasser wasn't oblivious to the fact that Anisa didn't want him near her. In fact, he'd anticipated some pushback from her. She wouldn't be the first obstinate client he'd had to handle in his line of work. Not everyone required the comprehensive physical and cybersecurity services his company, Sango Securities, provided, and those who did weren't always open to it. Part of his job was to ensure those resistant clients didn't wiggle away and come to harm under his watch. It was a burden Nasser could do without, and yet one he bore for the success of his business and the hundreds of employees who relied on him for their livelihoods.

So, no. Nasser wasn't surprised by Anisa's reaction to the news that her brother had hired him. It was even to be expected considering his arrival had come as a shock to her.

What did intrigue him was how she confronted him about it, getting up in his face…or as close as she could to his face given their notable height difference. That gave him pause in planning how to approach her. For every stubborn client who didn't believe his services were needed, Nasser strategized on how to appeal to their sensibilities. Whether it be stroking an ego or ingratiating himself to them, he did what he had to for his career and company. And in the six years since Sango Securities' inception, Nasser hadn't found a client he couldn't sway into becoming cooperative.

But his intuition warned him Anisa would be different. She wouldn't be like the philandering politicians, playboy millionaire heirs and other glitterati that made up the largest sum of his company's profit margin. Although an heiress to her family's shipping empire, and likely quite wealthy herself, Anisa proved markedly different the instant she squared up to him.

Normally Nasser wouldn't have taken the bait, but Anisa's defiance sparked a fire in him and provoked a response. The thrill of that clash unleashed something deep within him. Whatever it was hungered for another encounter like it, and that disturbed Nasser greatly. Particularly because despite seeming to have won their little argument, he couldn't shake the feeling that the battle was far from over.

She's going to try again.

Of that Nasser had no doubt. He saw it in the baleful way she would glance at him—*when* she deigned to look at him, that is.

He could see her mind puzzling out a scheme to wiggle free of his protection detail. It was truly impressive considering she worked nonstop while plotting against him simultaneously. Before meeting her, Nasser had done enough research to understand her job was film-industry-related. And though he hadn't seen a need to dig further into what she did for a living as it didn't seem to endanger her, from simple observation Nasser deduced she was an indispensable member of her team. With a headset glued to ears and a walkie-talkie clipped to her belt, Anisa was called on to do a number of tasks, running all over the grounds of the Rova. As the sun climbed higher and the dewy coolness of dawn yielded to a hotter late morning, Nasser marveled more at Anisa's endurance.

She never seemed to stop for very long, her sneakers burning rubber over the pavement as she accomplished one task and moved to the next. The only time she came to a rest was when she paused to cool off with a long pull from her water bottle. Yet juggling all that she was, Anisa still managed to carve out time to look daggers at him.

She's definitely plotting something...

Nasser sketched a mental note to beware her crafty mind *and* her surprising beauty.

The photos he'd seen of her, both the ones her brother had provided and the ones Nasser had collected from her social media accounts, didn't hold a candle to her in the flesh.

Anisa was very pretty, with her adorably small, turned-up nose, heart-shaped face, and soft, alluring mouth. It was wide and full, its heavier lower lip caught between her teeth whenever she was focusing on a task. Which was far too often.

Like yesterday, she was dressed simply in blue jeans and a plain long-sleeved shirt. But yesterday her hijab had been wrapped more classically over her head and neck. Today Anisa had styled it differently. The headscarf wound around her head in a simple turban, her slender brown neck left bare. He surmised that it was a way to keep herself cooler while she was rushed around.

He knew Anisa could easily have relied on her family's wealth and never had to work a day in her life, certainly not as hard as she was right then. Nasser commended her industrious spirit.

Admittedly, he was also relieved that Anisa was preoccupied as it gave him a chance to consider his strategy to win her over.

A stratagem he was confident would make her accept that it was pointless to fight him. That one way or another, Nasser would see through his protective detail until Anisa finished with her work in Madagascar and left for her home in Canada.

CHAPTER THREE

SEVERAL HOURS LATER, and Nasser's confidence had taken a hit.

Waiting for Anisa to finish working for the day so they could finally speak without interruptions had resulted in him following her around the city. Had Nasser known she would be working long hours, he might have reconsidered a better wardrobe and footwear.

He might even have rethought agreeing to this job.

Nasser sighed, knowing his decision to accept Ara's request to protect his younger sister had more to do with his own personal affairs than the big payday it offered. Money wasn't an issue in his life. He had millions to his name. But he was being paid with peace of mind.

Protect my sister, Ara had instructed him, promising, *In return, I'll help you find the men who killed your brother, Nuruddin.*

Nuruddin…

Nasser hadn't heard his brother's name mentioned in so very long. He knew that it was sadly the way things went when one passed away. Time eroded memories, names, faces. He hadn't expected to hear about Nuruddin from Ara. Anisa's brother was affording him a chance to finally track Nuruddin's killers. Because in spite of Nasser's wealth and powerful connections these days, vengeance was still one thing that eluded him. Vengeance for his brother. For their brokenhearted parents, who'd had to bury a son far too young.

And for myself. For the peace that could be mine, Nasser thought, the pain in his heart mingled with guilt.

He hadn't been able to save his brother—but this…revenge he could do.

Nasser lifted his head, closed his eyes and breathed in the city air, cooler at this late hour. When he opened his eyes again, he trained them on the expansive water before him.

Lake Anosy, with its jacaranda-lined shores, was a few miles away from Antananarivo's Upper Town, or La Haute Ville. Though still a frequented part of the city, it was far more peaceful a place to visit after a bustling day in the urban center of the capital. Of course, like most places, certain times of the day were less crowded. Right then, for instance, the setting sun cast long black shadows on the tree-lined trail along the shore. An isthmus connected the mainland to a small island in the manmade lake's center. The area boasted a tranquility that could quiet even the most anxious of minds.

He let that serenity in to clear his head until only a single thought remained: Anisa.

He hadn't forgotten that they still needed to chat. For him to do his job smoothly, he wanted her compliant. Her safety required a combined effort from them both. After all, if she insisted on placing herself in danger, Nasser could only do so much to protect her.

And if he couldn't protect her, then he could consider his job forfeit now.

Nasser frowned at the mere thought of defeat. He scowled more when he imagined the fight Anisa would put up.

So much for peace.

He spotted her easily amid a group of her coworkers, not far from where he stood under a fully blooming jacaranda tree. Her posture and expression were more relaxed now that she was officially off the clock. Though he couldn't hear what she or her crew members were saying, he watched a brilliant smile lift her cheeks, her mouth opening with laughter, her hand immediately flying over to catch the sound. He couldn't discern her mirth from the chatter of the group, and yet somehow he imagined the sound of her laugh would be something worth hearing and experiencing.

Why not right now? They were overdue a chat, and he hadn't endured twelve hours of her job to be deterred.

Fixing that to his mind, he made his move.

When he was within earshot, he caught another wave of laughter swelling from the group and dispersing into the evening air.

Aside from Anisa, who stood out to him the way an insect ventured to light even to the detriment of its well-being, the only other face he recognized was her little blonde friend. Darya, he believed she was called. He was still looking into her. The others, four males and one other female, were new to him. But since they were working alongside Anisa, Nasser would make it his business to search their backgrounds and ensure they posed no threats to her.

He tensed when one of the men flung an arm around Anisa's shoulders, pressed her to his side and lowered his head to angle his lips close to her ear.

Nasser narrowed his eyes at the point of contact, images of him ripping that arm off Anisa flashing into his mind unbidden.

And he might have succumbed to his baser urges if Anisa hadn't chosen that moment to roll her eyes at whatever he whispered into her ear. She drawled, "Hands off, Lucas," before elbowing him off her. She did it far more gently than he would have, but the elbow in the ribs did the trick in pushing away the unwanted advance.

With one final dark look at this Lucas who dared touch her, Nasser scrawled a mental instruction to have his diligent staff take extra time researching him especially.

Anisa looked past her circle of friends then, right at him.

Her eyes rounded in open surprise before she appeared to catch herself, furrowed her brows and pruned her lips.

Seeing no point in lurking in the umbrage of trees, Nasser stepped into the orange glow of the streetlights that illuminated Anisa and her co-workers.

"We need to talk," he stated, the announcement catching the attention of her friends. Unlike her, they hadn't noticed him yet.

Now that they did, their curiosity was flung from him to Anisa and back again.

Anisa visibly stiffened and crossed her arms, but she broke away from her group and walked up to him.

"After we talk, I will see you to your hotel," Nasser said and held his car keys up between them, hoping that his no-nonsense tone persuaded her.

"Fine."

She turned back and pulled her friend Darya aside. "I'm going to catch a ride with him." She pulled out her phone and added as if to goad him, "I'll send you a live location, you know, in case I go missing."

When she retraced her steps back to him, Nasser stepped in closer to her, and she took one sharp inhale in reaction.

"Good. I'm satisfied that you're endeavoring to protect yourself as well."

With her hijab styled as a turban, he could see her throat ripple in response to his words. Back-dropped by the purple blooms of the jacaranda— a tree whose flowers only bloomed in October and November—Anisa made for a mesmerizing portrait. It was one he cataloged for memory as his stare roved over the rosy-brown flush paint-ing the tip of her nose and the swell of her cheeks. The longer he studied her, the louder her breath-ing became in the silence, her lips parting for her quicker intakes of air. Fighting not to close his eyes, he subtly pulled in her natural scent min-gling with the blooming trees all around them. *Ya Allah.* But how could anyone smell so good? Feel-ing the same kind of breathlessness, he stepped off to the side, discreetly giving them the space they both seemed to need to concentrate.

As soon as he did, Anisa tightened her lips and flared her nostrils, huffing, "Your satisfaction wasn't my goal."

Masking his amusement at her comment, Nasser

jerked his chin toward his vehicle. "Follow me to my car."

Soon they were merged onto the road and driving back to the city's Upper Town, where her hotel was situated.

A direct route to her hotel would be about ten minutes, fifteen if nighttime traffic delayed them. Nasser expected their conversation needed no more than half an hour. So he would have to find more traffic than usual…

Beside him, Anisa tapped her shoes impatiently on the car floor. When he glanced at her, she speared him with an expectant look and crossed her arms.

"So, are you going to talk?" she asked briskly, all business.

Seeing no point in prolonging their inevitable conversation, at the next red light, Nasser fished for his wallet and retrieved a business card from it.

He set the card down on the center console between them. "Contact the number on the card to verify my credentials and identity. I wouldn't expect you to trust my word alone, even though you seem to already." His cheeky insinuation that she had trusted him without confirming that he was who he said he was didn't go unchecked. Anisa's glare came at him fast and fierce.

In hindsight, he could have worded that better, even if it bothered him that she'd let her guard down. As much as he would have liked to drill cautiousness into her, now wasn't the time or place. The objective was to get her to trust him enough to let him do his job of protecting her—

Not alienate her.

"You have my card now," he carried on, continuing as if her glower didn't have him on edge.

Holding out his card before her, she read, "Sango Securities."

"We're a private security firm."

"You're the boss?"

"I'm the founder and president."

Anisa sucking her teeth wasn't a good sign. "So, who's to say that your staff won't just lie about who you are?"

Once again she nearly pulled laughter out of him, the humor he fought to suppress twitching his lips and threatening to break his concentration. "You're right," he agreed hoarsely, still battling to regain control of his runaway mirth. "The reference from my staff won't be unbiased. There is another option, however: you could also always call your brother and ask him."

It wasn't the first time he'd proposed that she speak to Ara. Earlier when Nasser had suggested that she contact her brother, Anisa looked ready to strangle him with her bare hands. She had that same murderous slit to her eyes now.

"Why?" she asked frostily. "So you and my brother can team up against me?"

She might have said more, but her stomach chose that moment to grumble.

"You're hungry," he observed. "We can talk more over dinner—"

Anisa cut him off with an angry sniff. "No, I don't want dinner. What I *want* is for you to tell me what Ara is doing, and why whatever it is suddenly requires I need a bodyguard."

He could tell her, of course. About how he'd lost his older brother, Nuruddin, at an antigovernment rally over fifteen years ago, and that his life had never been the same since. Or perhaps he should be honest and come clean about knowing Anisa and her brother had lost their parents in a tragic boating accident—an accident that was no accident, but rather a staged double homicide targeting her mother and father. Ara hadn't spoken much on it, only that he suspected the same crooked government officials were behind the deaths of his parents and Nuruddin.

And that if Nasser were willing, he and Ara could join forces to avenge their lost family members.

He had been more than willing. It was why he was by Anisa's side now. Why looking her in the face, and knowing they were sharing a similar pain of losing people they loved, made it hard for him to utter lies.

She deserves to know, doesn't she?

Wavering, Nasser contemplated telling her the

truth of the quid pro quo deal he'd struck with her brother.

And what if telling her places her in danger?

It was the very reason why Ara had sworn him to secrecy.

My sister can't know anything about this deal of ours. I won't endanger her unnecessarily. Just make sure she gets home safely, and you'll have your names. You'll have your revenge.

Ara's vow ended Nasser's indecision.

"Well?" Anisa prompted him.

Nasser hated seeing the hope peeping out from her eyes. He watched the light fade when he shook his head. "Ask your brother. He simply hired my services. What he does isn't my business." Not an outright lie, but not also the truth. It was a middle ground he could live with.

Anisa's dark look could've fried him.

Unsurprisingly, she demanded, "Drop me off at my hotel, then, or I'll get out here and grab a cab."

Refusing to let her take a taxi, Nasser silently obeyed her first order, his jaws painfully clenched as he navigated traffic to her hotel. Once he parked in front of the hotel's entrance, Anisa hightailed it out of his vehicle.

Nasser moved quickly, exiting the car and catching her before she stomped away.

"You'll be here tomorrow, won't you? Because we can talk then."

For a split second, Anisa's anger blinked into

confusion. But by the time he noticed the shift in her mood, her features had flickered back to stone, and she jerked her head in what he presumed to be a nod. She didn't stick around after that, marching away into the hotel and leaving Nasser more drained than he'd felt in a long while.

Anisa couldn't immediately recall feeling that angry before.

She vibrated with rage all through the silent drive, half-relieved that Nasser hadn't tried again to speak to her. But the other half was annoyed that he had managed to maintain his composure while she felt seconds away from fracturing.

She resisted slamming his car door when he came to a halt at her hotel's entrance.

His car wasn't the true source of her crossness. *He is.*

Still, not wanting to bite his head off, she tried to storm away. But Nasser waylaid her briefly, questioning her work schedule. And she was too furious with him to do much else but nod. Fuming in her hotel suite now, she finally gave herself license to shout into the first pillow she could grab, but even that did little to dull her irritable mood.

This is just as much my fault.

Anisa had allowed him to get under her skin, and now she felt all out of sorts because of it.

Pushing away the pillow she'd screamed into, she flopped back onto the bed, glared up at the ceiling and racked her brain for a memory of when she'd been so riled by someone. The only other time she remembered being that upset was when Ara had reacted coldly to her desire to study and live abroad alone.

"Of course he's as annoying as Ara," Anisa groused. All of this circled back to her brother, and that just infuriated her more. What was with the men in her life and their all-consuming need for control? She couldn't see it any other way than Ara and Nasser not trusting her with their trifling secrets.

And she wouldn't be so bothered—

But they're disrupting my life!

Was she just supposed to sit there and accept it? That was a hard no, but what more could she do? Nasser's advice was for her to ask Ara…

Anisa's eyes nearly rolled right out of her skull.

If she thought she could ask Ara, she'd have never badgered Nasser in the first place. Not that he'd ever seemed flustered. Unlike her…

The memory of Nasser moving in closer to her at Lake Anosy less than an hour ago replayed in her mind. He'd filled her vision, the beautiful blossoming jacaranda and the lakeside view forgotten in lieu of him. Her brain then recreated the scene of their first showdown atop the Rova. Again, they stood so close that the encounter left an imprint on her. Every time, he had appeared unfazed to her, and that was almost as unfair as

Nasser holding on to her brother's secrets along with his own.

Even so, her anger started waning. The void it left behind filled with something curiously new...

She pressed her hands to her clenching belly, her insides churning more violently all of a sudden. Dismissing it as hunger would've been too easy. That wouldn't explain the heat wafting from her face or the delightful shivers rolling over her body. Chilled and overheated, she sat up in a daze, Nasser's stony yet darkly gorgeous face branded in her mind.

Was she feeling this way because of him?

With trepidation, Anisa tested her theory by closing her eyes and letting her imagination wander and wend its way back to him.

Opening her eyes, she moved her hands from her stomach up to her rabbiting heart.

Great. She had a crush on him. That didn't bode well for her willpower if she wanted to shake him loose.

Especially when Anisa sprang up to her feet at the sound of a knock on her front door, and her first thought was, *It can't be him.*

Seeing Darya brought equal measures of consolation and disappointment.

I'm only disappointed because he should have come to apologize.

"Hey," her friend greeted her, tilting her head in confusion. "You got back to the hotel before me. I was surprised to see the live location pinning you here, of all places. I'm guessing it didn't go well with your studly bodyguard?"

"Yeah, we didn't have much to talk about after all. Also, he's not *my* anything." Anisa emphasized the last part with a glare at Darya.

"Easy," Darya laughed, but when her humor abated, she asked, "All right. Tell me. What happened to put you in a bad mood?"

Anisa heaved a sigh. "Where do I start?"

She walked her friend through everything that had transpired with Nasser, starting with the business card he'd given her and ending on his poorly timed offer of dinner. At the end of her complaining, she anticipated a sympathetic ear.

Instead Darya looked his business card over and passed it back with a shrug. "Honestly, it just sounds like he's trying to do his job."

"A job I *don't want* him to do!" Anisa threw up her hands and groaned loudly. "I don't need to be babysat. What I really want is for my brother and Nasser to accept that."

"Right, but I can understand why they might think it's necessary."

"Please, enlighten me."

Darya snorted in disbelief. "Um, could it be the millions in your family?"

Not many people in her life knew about her family's wealth. Money her parents earned from their import-export business when they were alive, and now the money that her brother had successfully tripled—no, *quadrupled* since inheriting the shipping company their father and mother had begun years ago. When she'd first told Darya, Anisa had fully expected her friend to treat her differently. After all, they had initially bonded over their mutual love of film and being young immigrant women in their chosen industry. Darya had come from a poor background, migrating from eastern Europe to Canada all on her own in her late teens to provide for herself and her family back home. Although she was always careful not to show it, she must have been shocked to learn that Anisa was an heiress. Even if she was a reluctant one…

"All right, I can see your point," Anisa assented grudgingly. And before Darya could gloat, she hastened to add, "But I don't think that's why my brother hired Nasser. Don't ask me how I know. I just do."

Whatever Ara and Nasser were up to, her gut churned nauseously with a warning that their secrets were dangerous.

With that dark certainty in mind, she murmured, "If I didn't see or hear from either of them anytime soon, I'd be happy."

A sharp knock on the door interrupted them.

"Were you expecting a certain someone?" Darya eyed the door with a slow grin.

Anisa frowned, but her heart rate picked up as

she answered her second caller. It wasn't Nasser this time either, but one of the hotel's waitstaff. The young woman garbed in a maroon pantsuit held out a large white plastic bag and smilingly informed her, "A visitor left this for you at Reception." She passed Anisa the bag and along with it a folded note before strolling away.

Closing the door slowly, Anisa turned with her gaze trained on the note in her hand.

"Did someone leave you takeout?" Darya leaned closer and took a big whiff. "Mmm, smells heavenly."

Anisa had to agree that the divine smell coming from the bag revved up her hunger. But it was hard to concentrate on anything but the note that came with the takeaway meal. She set the bag down on the entryway table and dropped into the soft cushions of the sofa in the sitting area. Grabbing the spot next to her, Darya said nothing. Nevertheless, Anisa felt her impatience.

Overly anxious herself, she flipped open the note and saw the short message was written on the hotel's memo paper, but she quickly looked past the business letterhead to the few words inked neatly on the page in startlingly beautiful cursive:

I'm a man of my word, and I promised you dinner. I will see you tomorrow. Nasser.

She should have known—she suspected it was

him, but though unsigned, the note was confirmation.

He did come back.

And he brought her dinner, apparently. A dinner he hadn't, in fact, promised her. A dinner she'd walked away from in anger...

"It's Mr. Hot Bodyguard, isn't it?" Darya's soft voice broke the silence.

Anisa didn't even have the strength to argue that he wasn't hers.

She let Darya read the note then, getting up off the sofa to plate the takeaway dinner Nasser thoughtfully sent her. Anisa stopped when Darya walked over with the note.

"Wait. Doesn't he know that we're leaving Antananarivo tomorrow morning?"

Anisa bit her lip and looked down at the plate she'd filled with a steaming hot meat stew with fresh greens and accompanied by a side of white rice.

"You didn't tell him," Darya guessed.

"He seemed to think we'd still be here, and I didn't correct him." She shrugged. Their film crew was set to travel to different locations throughout Madagascar. That had always been the plan. "It's not an outright lie."

Just a lie of omission, she thought with a twinge of remorse not helped when Darya answered with a slow, disappointed shake of her head.

"Anisa, you have to tell him."

"Why should I?" She snapped her head up, a fire catching in her, the flames stoked by her ire at Nasser and Ara for leaving her in the dark over why she required protection. If they could have their secrets, why couldn't she do the same?

The guilt that momentarily had a hold on her melted.

It wasn't her fault that Nasser believed she would remain in Antananarivo tomorrow.

If he doesn't know I'm leaving, then he's just not that good of a bodyguard, Anisa reasoned.

And if he wasn't that good of a bodyguard, then Nasser had no business following her around, let alone protecting her.

CHAPTER FOUR

ANISA WOULDN'T EVER label herself a morning person, yet when her alarm woke her, she bounded out of bed with a smile and drew open the hotel's thick curtains to let in the golden beginnings of dawn brightening the dark sky.

After basking in the light of day, she showered and dressed, styled her hijab, prayed Fajr, and even had time to eat a proper breakfast—something she often forgot to do on her busiest workdays. Anisa didn't think too hard about her unusual burst of energy. She simply attributed it to a good night's sleep, which was rare for her when she was used to working twelve- to sixteen-hour shifts.

Her sunny mood stuck with her until she set foot outside her hotel, where she couldn't overlook the familiar black four-by-four in the circular drive or miss its very handsome driver leaning with his back pressed against the passenger door. His position gave him a straight view to the revolving entrance she stepped through.

Freezing in her tracks, she stared, disbelieving her eyes.

But Nasser didn't vanish.

Which means he's really standing there.

With that realization, all her good humor leaked away like a pricked balloon.

Anisa sucked in her lips, her mouth suddenly dry and her heart sounding in her ears. Squeezing her hand around the handle of her compact suitcase, she rolled it forward slowly, her steps echoing the hesitance that assailed her.

Drawing his sunglasses off when she came to a standstill a foot from him, Nasser fastened her with a searing look.

"Sightseeing early, or are we going someplace else?"

Anisa opened her mouth, then closed it, before opening it again in the hope that an appropriate excuse would come to her. Instead, grumbling car engines pierced the awkward quiet, and a minibus crawled up the drive. Closely following the bus was a mud-stained white four-by-four, older-looking than Nasser's vehicle. Both the minibus and four-wheel drive came to a stop behind Nasser's ride, and the driver's door of the minibus swung open.

"Anisa! Ready to go?" Lucas called to her, climbing out of the vehicle.

Acknowledging Lucas with a fearsome scowl, Nasser asked, "Where are you going, Anisa?"

He knows! How could he know?

Panic setting in, Anisa left her luggage standing on the drive and walked a little closer to Nasser.

"We're leaving Antananarivo. Our filming scheduling is tight, so we have to be on the road very soon." She swallowed hard, her gulp embarrassingly audible before she continued squeakily, "I...must have forgotten to mention it."

"I'm glad you told me now."

Anisa heard the smugness in his response and didn't even need proof of it from his unchanging, shuttered expression. He had known she lied, and he'd wanted her to confess to it. And she had... *Allah*, how could she be so oblivious? She walked right into that one! Now not only would she have to deal with the fact that he would follow her once again, but he'd caught her in a lie of her own making, a lie she couldn't even manage to conceal.

She glared at him to her own detriment, her temples pulsing warningly with a headache. Gritting her teeth against the dull pain, she closed her eyes and touched her fingers to the side of her forehead.

"Are you not feeling well?" Nasser's voice, though still notably deep and irritatingly unruffled in tone, sounded sharper than it had seconds ago.

Opening her eyes, Anisa blinked in wonder. Because it sounded like he actually cared...

Duh! Of course he does.

He was likely just worried for the sake of his job. Ara wouldn't be too happy if the bodyguard he hired had failed in protecting his precious little sister—even if it was only from a big, bad headache. Outside of that, she couldn't delude herself into thinking Nasser truly cared. And she had to be sure not to confuse concern that came with a price tag with real emotion.

"I'm fine," she said from between clenched teeth. Then she called to Lucas, "Make room for me."

She turned away from Nasser to grab her suitcase. Anisa hadn't made it two steps before she heard a commotion from the hotel's entrance and Darya calling to her.

"Anisa! Wait for me!"

Darya hurried toward Anisa and the idling minibus full of their crew members. She crowded closer to Anisa and dropped her voice while nudging her head sharply at Nasser, the fedora she'd purchased from the market nearly falling off from her obvious gesturing. "I thought you said you weren't going to tell him. Changed your mind?"

"He was here when I walked out," Anisa hissed. "He just knew. I don't know how, but he did."

Darya smiled blithely at him while murmuring, "Guess he's that good at his job." When Anisa groaned softly, her friend patted her arm reassuringly. "Well, you could ask him on the road."

Anisa shook her head slowly, letting those words sink in. "Wait. What do you mean, 'on the road'? I'm riding the minibus like everyone else."

"Yeah, about that…" Darya smiled sheepishly and pointed to the bellhop rolling a heavily laden luggage cart in their direction. There was a lot more there than when she and Darya had checked in two days ago. "After you left last night, Lucas drove the rest of us to the market again, and I *might* have gone a little overboard with purchases."

"A little?" Anisa's eyes bugged.

"I mean, I would go with your bodyguard—"

"He's not *mine*," Anisa interjected.

"But it's not like we know each other. That's why it would be better if you go." She chirped the last part happily, like the idea solved their problem.

Anisa watched hopelessly as Lucas and another crew member helped the bellhop haul Darya's belongings into the back of the minibus. She could see there was hardly any room left once Darya climbed in, mouthed *sorry*, and waved back at her. In desperation, she looked around at the four-by-four, but quickly saw that there would be no room for her there with the director and assistant director and their driver.

She heard Nasser before she felt him standing by her and saw his tall, imposing form in her peripheral.

He didn't say anything.

And it forced her to break their silence first. Though it killed her to ask him, she said, "May I please have a ride?" She bit her tongue when she wanted to add, "Since you're going to follow me anyways."

Anisa waited for him to drag this part out. Milk this moment for all it was worth. He hadn't only caught her in a lie; he was now her only option to follow her crew and continue to do her job. It was what she'd have done if their roles were reversed.

"I'll place your luggage in the trunk," he informed her.

Anisa craned her neck up and goggled at him, unclear if she heard him correctly.

"Or would you like to do it yourself?" He looked pointedly down at where her hand clasped her suitcase, her fingers practically glued to the handle from the way her knuckle bones protruded. She peeled her fingers loose. The instant she did, he grasped where her hand had been a heartbeat earlier.

Wordlessly, he pushed in the suitcase handle, hauled the hardcase roller up and forged a path to his vehicle.

No gloating followed.

That didn't mean her defenses weren't on alert. Anisa shadowed him slowly and cautiously, slid into the passenger seat beside him and looked for any signs that he was about to rub this in her face. Because surely, *surely* he wasn't doing any of this for sheer kindness's sake.

He's doing his job, so no. Not out of the kindness of his heart.

But Anisa couldn't figure out what angle he would come at her from. Would he annoy her throughout this long journey ahead, maybe make her wish that she hadn't omitted the truth of the trip? The only thing she could be certain of was that he wouldn't hurt her. Not if he was really working for Ara. Her brother wouldn't have sent anyone who lacked his implicit trust. And yet that didn't mean she trusted him not to be petty with her now.

She looked him over, his expensive suits traded in for a linen blazer, a buttoned oxford shirt and dark wash straight jeans. He hooked his sunglasses into the pocket of his blazer, his sleeves rolled up and the corded muscles of his forearm coming between them as he fiddled with the console screen.

"Would you like the radio on? Music, perhaps."

When she didn't respond, Nasser met her stare head-on. Having his full attention on her in the hush of his car and with no one else to witness whatever went down had a funny effect on her. First, her stomach flopped on her. And her headache was alive and well, but now her limbs were feeling quivery. If she hadn't known better, Anisa would've thought she was sicker than she actually was.

She had to be sick if she was noticing how soft and lush his lips looked, the way his jaw gleamed from what had to be a recent shave, and the decadent scent of his aftershave and cologne interspersed with the new leather smell coming from the car.

"Anisa."

Her name in his low, assertive voice had her sucking in a long breath, snapping to attention, and reminding herself that her little crush on him had no legs. Certainly not if he intended to force his company on her.

"Do what you want," she said with an indignant huff, then stared out the passenger window. "It's what you've been doing all along."

Nasser counted four hours since Anisa spoke to him last.

She hadn't said a word, not one, since they left Antananarivo on the freeway that would take them down south to where her film crew were scheduled to work next. Rather she sulked quietly, refusing to make eye contact or even acknowledge that he was sharing a tightly confined space with her, for better or worse.

He almost wished she would yell at him. Shout to her heart's content, get it out of her system and spare him the cold shoulder.

This is why you're not married—why you've given up on family.

Nasser knew that wasn't the entire truth of why he'd chosen celibacy over so-called wedded bliss. Being in a relationship meant that he provided for his intended life partner in every way. Caring for, loving, and protecting...

He had a problem with the protecting part most of all.

He hadn't been able to protect Nuruddin. Worse, he'd held his brother in his last moments and felt the life ebb from his body. Nasser shuddered at the memory, his heart a block of ice in his chest as he relived the worst day of his life.

If only we hadn't gone to that protest rally...

And if only Nasser hadn't left his brother's side when things had gotten dangerous and the local police and military hadn't used force to chase off protestors.

Breathing deeply, he wrung his hands on the steering wheel and forced himself back to the present, in the car with Anisa, as they drove down the long stretch of freeway. When he thought of Nuruddin, and of all the life experiences his brother would never get, Nasser knew the only thing that could make it right for him was abstaining from some of those experiences himself.

Hence his celibacy.

As excessive as it seemed, even if he were interested in a romantic relationship, he wouldn't be any good at it. Not if he couldn't protect those he loved.

So marriage just wasn't in his cards.

It's not my fate.

For some reason, as he thought this, he flung a glance at Anisa.

She had her back to him, her body angled toward the passenger door as though she intended to pop the lock and spring out of the car at a moment's notice. If that wasn't worrying, she also sat so still that he might have thought she was sleeping. Nasser frowned, not fooled. It was a tactic to avoid speaking to him.

He convinced himself that his annoyance was born simply out of frustration that came from the oppressive pall of silence that had befallen them.

He was relieved then when they finally reached a pit stop. The city of Antsirabe.

Following the lead of her crew ahead of them, Nasser finally pulled in to park in front of a large, picturesque colonial building, the architectural touches a nod to the bygone Belle Epoque. Just as fascinating, the city teemed with colorful rickshaws. Nasser had dodged several of the man-powered vehicles as he navigated into the central part of the town.

As soon as he cut the engine, Anisa unfurled from her seat, unlocked her seat belt and opened her door first.

She can't wait to run from me.

Nasser silenced that mental poison before the line of thinking bought him trouble. What Anisa did wasn't his problem unless it risked her safety. Like when she waved to her friend Darya from across the street and bolted into the road after looking both ways only once.

She missed the motorbike that careened around the corner. Nasser acted fast, caught her arm and hauled her back into him. The propulsion jerked her to his chest. He immediately and instinctively wrapped his arms around her. He breathed heavily, watching the bike roar past the spot Anisa had just been standing, and fought back the tragic image of what could have been her broken body lying on the street.

It might have explained why he held on to her longer than was necessary.

Why it had gotten to the point where he felt her physically stiffen in his hold and then press her hands to his chest and push back against him.

But she didn't step away when he lowered his arms and she dropped her hands off him. Anisa peered up at him, just as she had every other time they stood nearly toe-to-toe, standing off against each other.

It's different this time…

Nasser had breached her personal space—and yes, it started because he'd wanted to save her, *protect* her from herself if need be. But what happened after, his panicked visual of her dying on him, and then holding her past the point of rationality, that would be tougher to explain.

Rather than demanding he do just that, Anisa stared at him, in no hurry, it seemed, to order answers from him.

"Are you all right?" he asked gruffly.

She hummed as if agreeing, but the dazed look on her face didn't give him confidence that she had heard him, let alone comprehended what he'd asked her.

Who knew how long they stood there? It had to be a while for her friend to have reached them and yank Anisa away from him into a fierce hug.

"Oh, my God! Did you see that maniac driver? You almost got run over."

"I'm fine, Darya. Really." Anisa soothed her friend and patted her back, but her gaze remained wholly his.

She didn't break eye contact with him until Darya forced her to repeat the assurance that she hadn't come to harm.

Nasser quietly freed the breath he'd held the instant she left the safety of his car.

He itched to get her back there, where he could be assured no harm could come to her, but he knew that it would have to wait until her crew members were finished taking their break in the city.

"Come on." Pulling on Anisa's hands, Darya gestured to their crew and cast across the street, everyone having piled out of the minibus and the dusty white four-by-four. "We're all heading to lunch together."

Anisa's eyes locked on Nasser again, an indecisiveness to the way she looked at him.

A car horn blared.

The man Anisa had called Lucas tapped the horn of the minibus again and waved his arm at them.

"Are you beautiful ladies coming or what?" he hollered, getting the crew laughing at his antics.

Nasser twisted his mouth, aggravated at the recall of Lucas touching Anisa, and the fact that if she walked away now he wouldn't be able to follow her to lunch. He wasn't a member of her crew or cast. And so he'd be forced to remain outside whatever restaurant they chose, where he'd be prowling like a caged beast marking the boundaries of its prison, searching desperately for escape.

That image wrested a memory from the gloomiest recesses of his mind.

It was of him in a lightless, constricted hole of a place, the cold gust of night whistling through the bars and knifing through the thin, worn material of his shirt and pants, and the sole source of heat from the other bodies crammed into the jail cell.

He never, ever wished to feel that weak and powerless again.

If that meant Nasser had to choke down the fiery helplessness creeping up his throat at the thought of watching from the outside while Anisa lunched with her friends and coworkers, then so be it.

But his ears perked up when Anisa said, "Go without me." She didn't look back after Darya shrugged, said her temporary farewell and crossed the street. Before long, Anisa's crew and the cast members strolled off down the street in search of a meal.

It left them alone once more.

"You stayed," he observed, not permitting himself to dwell on the buoyant turn of his mood now that Anisa remained by his side.

She gave him an eye roll. "I *stayed*, yes, but don't get it twisted."

"Twisted?"

"Confused," she explained.

"Why would I be confused?"

For a moment she simply stared. Then, shaking her head as if clearing her mind, she said, "We should try talking again."

Try as he might to quiet it, that odd effervescence only jangled louder in Nasser. Giving up, he nodded. They hadn't gotten the chance to speak last time. Anisa had hurried off on him—

That's after I didn't give her the answers to secrets she wanted.

Nasser silently vowed to be gentler in his refusal this time. Though he wasn't willing to tell her the reasons he'd entered her life, he also wouldn't offer Anisa a chance to get upset with him. Somehow, he'd find a way to keep her happy without burdening her with problems that were his and Ara's.

"Lunch is on you though." Anisa raised her voice to be heard over the busy city noises as she marched ahead.

With her back to him, Nasser indulged in a smile and murmured, "Lunch should be interesting, then…"

CHAPTER FIVE

"*ÇA VA?*"

It was the second time Nasser had asked after her health, and Anisa couldn't be annoyed, not after he'd saved her from being plowed over by that reckless motorbike driver. To think she'd been a heartbeat away from becoming one big stain on the pavement—

She squeezed her eyes at the horrid image that last thought conjured.

If Nasser hadn't been there…

She still felt his arms around her, his hands poised at her back, holding her to him while the imminent danger passed them by. Because of his quick actions, he'd rescued her from grave injury.

Possibly death.

A shudder raked through her. Now that the adrenaline had ebbed from her system, residual fear left her shaken up, and anxiety pressed down on her chest. Her next few breaths sawed out fast and almost painfully.

They were walking together, Nasser placing

himself between her and the street. And yet every car passing had her nearly jumping out of her bones.

Funny. She'd thought she was doing fine enough, but it seemed that the initial shock had held her real fright at bay. Suddenly she couldn't think of anything else except that she'd almost just died.

Ears ringing and heart drumming, Anisa hadn't realized she'd been walking faster until Nasser's hand came out of nowhere and alighted on her arm. Startled by his sudden touch, she stopped dead in her tracks and looked up at him wide-eyed.

Meeting his gaze only reminded her of the close brush with fatality she'd just had.

"Anisa, you didn't answer me. Are you all right? Because if you're not doing well, I would like to know." He spoke with such authority. It should have rubbed her wrong, but the unconcealed concern in his voice and the strain of it in his expression dispelled her irritation.

"I'm fine," she murmured, not sounding at all like she was fine.

"Can you walk a little further? Otherwise, use my arm and lean on me."

Anisa's snort and eye roll had her feeling more like herself. Shrugging his hand off her arm, and ignoring the tingling heat his touch had left behind on her, she said, "I think I can make it, thanks," and forced herself to walk away from him.

He wasn't far behind her when he gestured across the street and instructed her to switch directions.

"We'll ride *le pousse-pousse* from here. It will be quicker."

Anisa wanted to ask what a *pousse-pousse* was, but she had her answer when Nasser crossed the street with her and stopped in front of a rickshaw, its gleaming red body, blue roof, wheel spokes and rims all looking freshly painted.

The rickshaw driver awaited them, his smile stretched wide as he flagged them over to take a seat.

Nasser spoke in rapid French to him. Anisa didn't even bother to follow whatever was being said, simply interpreting that they must have come to some deal in the end. Nasser then offered her a hand she didn't refuse and helped her to a seat on the hard but sturdy black bench of the rickshaw. He climbed in beside her. The driver crouched low, gripped the handles of the carriage and lifted them with an ease that belied his thin, wiry build and ashy bare feet.

As interesting an experience as it was, it wasn't the mode of travel that she would have chosen right then with her stomach in knots and her head lightly pounding with an impending headache. Anisa held on to the side of the rickshaw, her fingers taut and her body tensing in preparation to be rocked back and forth.

Surprisingly, the ride was smooth.

Pleasant, she thought with a faint smile, tilting her head to the breeze that now stirred over her face.

Nasser didn't miss it, not with the way he kept his eyes on her. But he didn't broach the subject of her well-being for a third time, and Anisa was grateful for it, not really wanting to relive having nearly been flattened by a motorbike. She just wanted to forget it ever happened.

She shut her eyes for what felt like a second before rousing at the feel of warmth on her shoulder. She saw Nasser retracting his hand, so she figured he had woken her after she'd accidentally fallen asleep. The rickshaw had come to a stop. He wasn't sitting by her anymore either. Standing outside the rickshaw on her side, he proffered his hand for her to climb out.

They stood before what she presumed was their intended destination, a restaurant with a lovely terrace view.

Nasser found them a table on the elevated terrace, pleasing her with his choice. The instant she saw the outdoor seating, she'd wanted nothing more than to sit down, enjoy a meal and soak in the postcard-pretty vista. She didn't even mind that Nasser helped her order. He had the decency to let her point out what she wanted from the menu and translated whatever French on the laminated pages stumped her.

Their drinks arrived, and she heeded him when he passed her a glass and commanded, "Drink. You had a shock."

Anisa expected the creamy beige concoction to taste sweet, but she was unprepared for the tangy punch to her taste buds. She pulled a face, and Nasser set a second glass by her. This one was plain ice-cold water.

"What did I just drink?" She pointed to the glass, the beverage still thick on her tongue. Though it was cool, and not terrible in taste, her pounding head and empty stomach hadn't appreciated the saccharine kick to her mouth.

"Baobab juice. It's milled from the seed of the baobab trees that are local to this area and along the island. It's a quick fix to elevate your sugar levels, but if it's not to your taste, I could send for the menu and you could pick something else."

Anisa regarded the baobab juice with renewed interest. She wouldn't mind having another sip, but she needed something in her stomach before she was willing to try again.

"Maybe I should have a real meal first."

Nasser smiled. A genuine smile that didn't disappear when she blinked and looked closer to see if she imagined it. As he called a waiter over, it stayed put on his handsome face, adding an extra layer of attractiveness. Now she had to sit across from him and endure the detrimental effect his dashing good looks had on her.

Anisa's stomach swished nervously at that.

But she didn't let it stop her from blurting, "Why are you being so nice to me?"

It wasn't just that he saved her from being road-kill. He hadn't once tried to hold her earlier lie over her head, and now all this concern for her well-being. She didn't know what to make of it.

"You know I lied to you about leaving Anta-nanarivo, right?" she continued, her word vomit not seeming to have an end. If she weren't so be-wildered by his displays of kindness, Anisa might have had the sense to be embarrassed. "I didn't want you to follow me."

"I figured as much." Nasser's smile was gone, but there was a humor and ease to his tone.

"And that doesn't piss you off?"

"Piss me off?" he echoed, looking lost in trans-lation.

"*Angry*. Doesn't what I did—*how* I've been act-ing upset you?"

Nasser tipped his head slightly. "You already made it obvious that my presence isn't wanted, and your behavior is consistent with that fact. So, what reason would I have to be angry?"

"I would be," she muttered.

"Upset or not, my duty is to protect you."

"Is that why you won't tell me the reason I need protection?"

The long, heavy breath he heaved could have rattled their table and the tableware along with it. Nostrils still flared with his exasperated sigh, Nasser said, "Not all danger comes in the form of a careless driver on the road. Sometimes knowledge can be just as threatening. The difference is that at least if you're run over, you might stand a chance of being put back together. But what you learn is harder to undo."

"So," she drawled, "that's your way of saying that I'm better off not knowing anything."

"I only say it because it's true." His face grew harder with his warning.

Anisa expected to be disappointed and irritated by his non-answer. Strangely though, she didn't mind that he stonewalled her again.

At least he actually spoke to me this time.

It was progress—and progress equaled hope that she was a bit closer to uncovering how her safety was connected to Ara's and Nasser's secrets.

She's safe.

If he repeated it enough times, it was possible Nasser might finally believe it to be true.

But then he grimly thought, *For now, she's safe.*

The question that eluded him was, for how long? And despite convincing evidence that Anisa was not in harm's way, he couldn't rise above the blame holding him down, shackling him in emotional fetters.

Couldn't let it pass that she'd almost gotten mortally wounded, killed even, and on his watch.

See your worthlessness? an insidious little voice hissed from somewhere inside his head. *You can't protect the things that matter. The* people *that matter. You don't deserve happiness.*

Nasser shook his head—and still the voice attacked, chipped at him, echoed the sentiment that he held no value, no true worth if he couldn't protect what was his.

And right now, whether she wanted to get rid of his protection services or not, Anisa was *his*.

His to safeguard. *His* until his job ended.

Mine for now. Mine.

He considered her with that possessiveness coursing through him. Anisa looked and sounded better. That was the important thing. After they left the restaurant, she even insisted on riding back in a *pousse-pousse* to reunite with her crew before they left Antsirabe. Crushed together in the rickshaw, Nasser held still to avoid touching her any more than they were forced to in the restricted space. Anisa didn't seem to care, because she was shifting in her seat and craning her head out from under the rickshaw's roof to take in the passing sights.

"I wish we could stay here and explore," she muttered to herself, but loud enough for him to pick up on.

"Why doesn't your crew film in this city? It's supposed to be quite the tourist trap. A spa town set in the sublime highlands of Madagascar."

Anisa's sigh drifted over to him. "We're on a schedule, that's why. We won't finish filming if we stop every other place."

"And what is it that you do exactly?" He hadn't missed how hard she worked. Surely she must be a crucial member of her team.

"I'm a production assistant," she said, surprising him with that reply.

He wasn't going to judge her skill or merit based on her job title, but a production assistant was an entry-level position. Intrigued, Nasser asked, "Is this a job you wanted to do?"

"Honestly? Not really. It pays the bills, and I get to work with film, but it's not what I finished school to accomplish."

"What do you want to do?"

Anisa pierced him with a look and harrumphed, the sound adorably ruffled. "What's with the interrogation?" She straightened her posture and turned her body to confront him, and he saw where her thinking had headed. "Are you sending this information back to my brother? Is that why you're so curious about what I'm doing?"

Nasser fought to keep his face straight. He didn't think she would appreciate him laughing at her, even though her accusation was laughable.

"I swear that your brother isn't in my ear. Just because he hired me doesn't mean he's privy to a conversation with my client."

"And I'm now a client?"

"In a way, you are."

"Even if I don't want to be," she grumbled, folding her arms and drawing her legs back to her side of the rickshaw.

They had just spoken about this in the restaurant, and Nasser had fervently hoped that he'd finally gotten through to her that some secrets were better off remaining secrets. Before he could worry that she would try to pelt him with more questions that would weaken his defenses against her, Anisa blew a long breath and rolled her shoulders as if to rid herself of tension.

"Okay, so you're a bodyguard for a living. What does that entail? You know, besides forcing your protection on people who don't want or need it."

Nasser's lips hitched up. He rarely found occasion to smile, but with Anisa he'd done it frequently.

"You have my business card, but essentially I run a corporate security company. Everything from physical security and cyber to natural disasters, we provide our clientele with the means to protect what matters to them most."

Anisa's snort could be heard from a mile away. "That can't be right."

"It's our company motto."

"Doesn't make it right," she quipped, her humor laced with bitterness. "Because there's no possible way that applies to *my* brother."

It was how she said it that had him sitting up

straighter, his jaw hardening and his brows slamming down. "What do you mean?"

"I don't know what my brother has led you to believe, but I don't matter to him."

"Why would you say that?"

Anisa whipped her head to him, her eyes ablaze and her voice quavering angrily. "If I really was so important to him, if my safety was truly his only worry, he wouldn't have sent you. He'd be here himself."

Nasser sat back, the force of her words and the emotional pain behind them slamming into him. He had sensed there was some undefined strain in Ara and Anisa's relationship. Although her brother hadn't mentioned it specifically, when Ara had requested this protection detail from Nasser—the last time they'd spoken—he had hinted at some tension with Anisa.

Wouldn't it be easier and far less costly for you to go yourself? Nasser had asked.

Ara had given him a tired look. *She won't want to see me.*

It didn't seem that way to Nasser. In spite of whatever might have caused the rift between the siblings, it was obvious to him that Anisa would have welcomed Ara. Perhaps not warmly at first, but she wouldn't have turned him away.

"You must have a reason to think that way," he said.

Anisa sniffed and shifted, as if she couldn't look him in the eye while she spoke.

"Again, I'm not sure what Ara's told you about us, but we haven't spoken for years."

Years?

Nasser brooded on her confession, wondering what had transpired for them to not speak for so long.

"Four years almost, next month. No texts, no calls. He just completely cut me out of his life, and for what?" She scoffed. "To assert his control, prove that I somehow need him more than he could ever need me. He was always smarter, more adaptable, and far more reliable than me. What use could I be to him?"

Rather than insisting it couldn't be true, knowing that was probably the last thing she wanted to hear, Nasser instead said, "If you haven't spoken for four years, how does he know so much about you?"

Anisa barked a short, bitter laugh. "Are you sure you've met Ara? I wouldn't be surprised if he had people following me." Continuing on a softer, sadder note, she told him, "I might not have the resources that he does, but I've tried to be a part of his life too. A family friend keeps me updated. Adeero Sharmarke is my only connection to my brother and our home."

Having done his own research on Anisa's and Ara's backgrounds, Nasser knew this Sharmarke.

A statesman in the Somaliland government and a tribal leader or *suldaan* of a larger local clan, this man she called her *adeero* wasn't truly her uncle by blood. On top of sharing the same tribal bloodline, Sharmarke had been schoolmates and work colleagues with Anisa and Ara's late father, Abdulwahab.

Though they had been friends, unlike Anisa's father, Sharmarke was of a nationalistic mindset. Which meant he hadn't been a supporter of Abdulwahab's idea to expand his homegrown shipping business through a partnership with interested foreign parties from China to Turkey. The Indian Ocean had long held the interest of many international investors. If Nasser were in the business of import-export, he'd have considered international trade contracts and building new ports.

Yet there were some like Sharmarke who didn't see it that way. Who instead worried that inviting outsiders to a piece of the Somali coastline was a sure way to losing nationalistic independence. And Sharmarke was a powerful man, with money and connections he wasn't shy to use to further his political values and goals.

He hadn't ever asked, but Nasser often wondered how Sharmarke and Ara saw eye to eye, especially since Ara had taken up his father's legacy and actively sought to open their waters to a wider global market.

I can't imagine they do see eye to eye.

But Ara and Sharmarke weren't his concern. Anisa was. And she sat with her hands folded in her lap, her melancholy a living, breathing entity that shared the rickshaw ride with them. Without needing her to clarify, he could see the weight this strife with Ara dealt her. And for some reason, that inspired unfriendly thoughts from him toward Ara. Why was he making his sister suffer needlessly when one word of true acknowledgment from him could spell a world of peace for her?

Nasser clenched his fists and locked his jaw tighter as he silently questioned, *Why put her through this pain?*

Feeling the rickshaw slowing compelled him to speak while they were still alone together.

"Whatever you may think, your brother doesn't wish harm to befall you. Otherwise he wouldn't have hired me."

"We'll have to disagree on that," she said with a weary glance at him.

And with inconvenient timing, their rickshaw came to a standstill right behind his four-wheel drive. Their driver lowered the vehicle so they could exit safely. Anisa alighted and returned a wave to her friend Darya. The crew were gathered across the street, back where they started when they first entered Antsirabe.

Intent on finishing their conversation, Nasser

descended from the rickshaw beside Anisa and gazed down at her growing frown.

"We disagree then. But never doubt that your welfare matters to me."

There. He'd made his sentiment known. Expecting her to leave now, Nasser waited for her to hurry off to Darya and the crew members loading back into their vehicles. He was even prepared for her to find room on the minibus and ride along with them rather than continue the final leg of their journey to their destination with him.

After what seemed like a moment of vacillation, she veered for his car. Dumbfounded, Nasser followed her jeans molded tightly to her swishing hips, his bemusement quickly devolving into a crackling whip of heat that lashed him out of the blue. And he didn't have to wonder what she would feel like, having held her curves himself not too long ago, his palms reliving the pleasant sensation of that too-brief contact and his body feverish from yearning for another chance to hold her.

No. He gave his head a good, solid shake to right his broken concentration. Anisa was off-limits, for so many reasons he couldn't begin to number them.

Meeting her there, Nasser unlocked the car doors and joined her inside.

"I thought you would have gone with your co-workers," he remarked coolly, still unclear why she had chosen his company again, like she had for lunch.

"It's still a possibility."

He scowled.

Her teasing smirk indicated that she saw his displeasure. "I might be persuaded to stay. Do I get to choose the music this time?" They'd listened to his songs from Antananarivo. It was a small price to pay to fulfill her request and appease her. But had she asked for more, Nasser admitted to himself that he would have been tempted to give Anisa whatever she asked of him, including his secrets.

He should be thankful it was only the music she desired for now…

For the second time in a day, Anisa awoke to Nasser's touch, only this time his face hovered close to hers.

He pulled back from the open passenger window once her eyes fully focused on him, the haze of slumber clearing from her vision.

"You asked me to wake you when we arrived."

"And we did?" Anisa yawned, covering her mouth and stretching her arms. She unfastened her seat belt and mumbled her gratitude when he opened the car door for her. He was looking at her with that single-minded intensity again, and her skin prickled with goose bumps, a tantalizing shiver trembling over her limbs.

When Nasser didn't stop staring, she wiped at her face, fretting that there was eye goop from sleep crusted on her eyes and drool dried on her chin.

"Is there something on my face?" she blurted, her cheeks warming.

"Non."

"Then why are you looking at me like I've grown two heads?"

A look of understanding chased over his face before he turned from her.

Like he didn't realize he was staring...

Anisa didn't know what to make of that. To her it appeared as if his actions surprised even him— but that didn't seem possible, not when Nasser presented himself as a man in control of everything in his world, with his emotions under wrap.

Lucky for him, she soon forgot all about what she had witnessed in lieu of the natural beauty surrounding them.

"Oh! It's so beautiful," Anisa breathed, her awe racing out of her.

All the pictures of the Alley of the Baobabs hadn't done the place justice, for it was far more magical in person. The dark silhouettes of the baobab trees, their root-like branches blotting out the glittering stars winking awake in the sky, created a hauntingly beautiful portrait. She pulled her phone out, glad she'd recently treated herself to a hardware upgrade, and snapped some photos.

Of the light leaching from the sky, of dusk sweeping over the long baobab-lined road, and then the lens of her phone camera trained on Nasser.

He stood as still as the tall, ancient trees rooted around them, a pensiveness in his side profile as he cast his eyes over the horizon, guarding against the troubles that might be lurking in the oncoming night.

The natural lighting worked well for him, and she couldn't resist taking a photo. She didn't have the flash on and managed to sneak the shot. Then another. She grabbed two more photos of him before he suddenly swiveled his head to her, his chiseled features emotionless and yet calling to her so that she nearly dropped her phone, her trembling hands lowering before she did.

"Did you take a picture of me?"

"I might have." She waited for him to ask her to delete it, and when he didn't, she offered, "I could send it to you. You looked good."

Nasser muttered something in French and then glanced away, his head tipping back and his eyes searching the skies.

"I didn't take you for a stargazer," she said, fascinated by this other side to him.

"I'm not. My brother was."

Stunned into silence by that small but significant reveal, Anisa's shock morphed into sadness when realization struck her.

Was. Rather than *is.*

He'd used the past tense. It only meant one thing: his brother was no longer with them.

Grief for him constricted her heart and had her eyes welling up. Nasser didn't even seem aware of what he'd told her, his focus on the stars. Concerned, she recognized that faraway look in his eyes more intimately than she wished she had. It was the look that preceded the spiral of emotions that sometimes followed whenever she thought of her lost parents. Nothing good ever came of it. And leaving him to be dragged deeper into his misery wasn't an option.

So she said the first thing that came to mind. "Earlier you asked me what I really want to do for a living."

When Nasser didn't look at her, she babbled, "A writer. I want to be a screenwriter. Tell stories that others want to bring to life on a big screen, or heck, even a theater's grand stage."

He angled his head down to her finally, his face unreadable but his eyes clearing of any lingering gloom.

Somewhere behind them, the general crew call sounded.

"I should go to work before they notice I'm missing," she said with a timid smile.

Nasser inclined his head.

Anisa took a few steps from him before whirling back. "Thank you."

"For?" he wondered hoarsely.

"For saving me." She hadn't given him his due gratitude yet, though she'd been meaning to. He had protected her when she needed it, not only from the motorbike, but from the despair that arose when Anisa had discussed her tense relationship with Ara. Nasser had made for a surprisingly good sounding board. Ironic, because he was determined to ignore the fact that she didn't *want* a bodyguard.

I might not want one...

But maybe, aside from all her complaining, *maybe* she could use one.

CHAPTER SIX

"If we'd wrapped a second later, I would have fallen over," Anisa griped to Darya the next morning, another early one. The only upside was that they'd filmed a sunrise in the Avenue of the Baobabs. Watching the starry sky dull and the nighttime fog lift as daybreak bathed the landscape was as much a pleasure as it had been to watch the sun set on that mystical corridor of baobab trees.

Yawning loudly and blinking away the tears of fatigue from her eyes, Anisa followed her crew to the minibus with the last of their set equipment. Their director and assistant director climbed into their four-by-four rental. She freed herself of her walkie-talkie last and then stretched, another powerful yawn raking through her body and curling her toes.

What she wouldn't give to find the closest bed so she could shut out the world for a few hours.

Her nose twitched. She lowered her arms from her stretch, straightening her blouse and sniffing the air. She turned and discovered Nasser holding out a paper cup to her, the aroma of strong black coffee wafting from the cup. It was a welcome scent after a series of early mornings and long workdays.

"Thank you," she moaned after that first sip transported her to nirvana.

A few more sips grounded her, and she had the sense to notice he also offered her a small plastic bag. The last time he'd sent her a bag, it was full of a tasty dinner she had shared with Darya.

She juggled her coffee and peeked into the bag, her eyes closing at the mouthwatering fried scent that teased her nose.

"The shopkeep called them *mokary*," Nasser told her.

"They look like tiny pancakes." She plucked one of the fried cakes from the bag and popped it into her mouth, chewing and delighting in the light sweetness coming from a creamy coconut flavoring.

They walked their makeshift breakfast to his car, where he showed her how to dip the delicate *mokary* into the bitter coffee and savor the robust fusion of textures, flavors and tastes. She might have been embarrassed to be moaning so much, but her hunger didn't have the sense to be humiliated. And it was hunger talking when she polished off the last *mokary*, looked into the empty bag sadly and reported, "There's no more left."

"We can get more when we head back into

town," promised Nasser, starting his engine and gearing the car into Drive.

Anisa shook her head, her moan now full of dread. "Don't remind me. We'll barely have enough time to eat before we're back on the road again."

"Where are you all headed now?"

"Are you asking because you don't know, or because you want to confirm what you know already?" Anisa grinned when Nasser's gaze strayed from the road to regard her. "I'm only teasing. We're going to Nosy Be. It's supposed to be this island paradise, a real touristy spot. The pictures online looked heavenly..."

"That's far north," Nasser reported with one of his many frowns. "How is your crew planning to get up to Nosy Be?"

"Let me check our call sheet." She flipped through her phone for the all-important file. "The notes from the assistant director say that we're traveling up the west coast before we go back on the highway to Antananarivo again."

"The backroads up the west coast won't be safer."

"But we save an hour or two on the road," Anisa said, tapping her phone screen when she compared the routes on her map app. Then she snapped her head up. "How do you know the roads won't be safe?"

"The shopkeep who made the coffee and *mo-*

kary explained as much. Some of these rural areas are unpoliced, and banditry is sometimes an issue."

Well, that proved what she suspected. He already knew what route they would be taking.

"I'm sure we'll be fine," she said.

He grunted something in French. It sounded like he replied, "We'll see."

Nasser used every second after they left L'Allée des Baobabs and stopped in at the small coastal town of Morondava once more to plan a safer route of travel for Anisa and her crew.

He made calls and got the ball rolling on the solution he'd formulated in that time. It included pulling the director and assistant director aside and making them an offer they couldn't refuse.

And once everyone was ready to go a couple hours later, Nasser listened in as the new plan—his plan—was announced.

He didn't even mind that the director and assistant director took credit when the crew and cast oohed and aahed their way through the announcement that they would be taking a private jet from Morondava Airport to Antananarivo before flying out from Tana to their island destination.

"Did you have something to do with this?" Anisa said with her hands poised on her hips once the rest of her crew was out of earshot on the tarmac. Then she kissed her teeth and dropped her hands. "Actually, don't tell me. I don't want to know." He followed her to his plane, smiling and greeting the pilot, copilot and two flight attendants at the base of the airstairs.

The tour of the plane cabin kept the cast and crew busy. Anisa joined in, but she kept glancing at him, looking away whenever their eyes clashed.

Eventually she claimed the seat beside him, making it easier for Nasser to watch over her. Anisa turned to face him, her elbow perched on the armrest between them, hand curled under her chin, an inquisitiveness furrowing her brow. "Tell me, what does a man do with so much space?"

"Mostly? Business meetings on the go. Rarely, we use them to transport clients out of…difficult situations."

"Hostage negotiations?"

His lips quirked at her imagination, even though it wasn't far from that really.

"Do you know how bad these big jets are for the environment?"

"I'm aware. Our company incorporates and employs environmentally conscious practices, and we partner with a company that specializes in sustainable aviation fuel. We also only use the plane in special cases."

"Of course you do," she said. "But do you really need glass room dividers—" she pointed to the divider separating a dining space "—the crystal chandeliers, a massive bed, and—is this real gold?" She rubbed her hand over the gold accent lining the buttery cream-colored leather of her armrest.

"I believe it is," Nasser murmured, pretending to be unaffected as her breath hitched and her fingers carefully grazed over the sleek gold touches. It reminded him of when he'd made his first million several years ago. The disbelief at having that much money to call his own had floored him. Now that he had it several times over, the novelty had long worn off, and yet he still counted his blessings every day. He was lucky—

Nasser wished he could say the same for his brother. Nuruddin's death seemed more than unfair. It sometimes felt like a mistake. He should have been taken, not Nuruddin.

Why did he die and I live? Not only had he lived, but he'd thrived. *Why me?*

He often posed that question to the universe, and he hadn't gotten an answer back yet. Wearying of those thoughts, he concentrated harder on Anisa and amused himself with her soft gasp of awe as she tipped her seat to lie back. He bit back a laugh when she sighed happily, closed her eyes and exclaimed, "Okay, I think I like this part the best."

A primal pride thumped in his chest in time with his heart. He'd put that blissful smile on her face.

And she put one on his when she cracked open

an eye. "Don't get me wrong. I still think the jet is absurdly big."

"You should see your brother's yacht."

"His *what*?"

Nasser heard the bristling anger in her voice and knew he'd stuck his foot in his mouth. It wasn't often that he spoke without thinking, but now that it had happened, he saw the negative effect of it unfold on Anisa's lovely face. Shock and fury warred with hurt. The latter struck him the hardest, pained him the most.

You fool, he berated himself.

He had worked hard over the past couple days to get in her good graces, and in a few words he'd undone all that effort.

Anisa pushed the button to raise her seat, then glared at him. The power of her fierce stare demolished any excuses he could to evade her curiosity.

"Of *course* he has a yacht! Let me guess, it's a floating manor," she hissed.

Nasser hazarded a look back at her crewmates. As he'd requested earlier, the flight attendants served freshly prepared snacks from the full kitchen to Nasser's guests before they completed the preflight checks. Though everyone seemed preoccupied, he would've preferred having his chat with Anisa someplace else. And he knew such a place.

"Come with me," he said low and bluntly. Not

waiting for her response, Nasser drew himself to a stand and headed for the business lounge.

Behind a solid partition, the lounge was comprised of a long conference table that could comfortably seat twelve. A large, ultra-high-definition flat screen television floated behind the head of the table, and there was a built-in credenza for refreshments if business meetings stretched long.

The partition would give them some privacy from the chatter and laughter floating in from the main cabin area.

As Anisa stalked closer to him, Nasser could see what she was thinking, and so he cut ahead of her.

"I apologize for being so brusque, but I thought we'd be more comfortable here." He sensed the privacy was something they both could use right then.

"A yacht!" Anisa threw her hands up, her scoff loud and high and quaking with emotion. "I can't believe I'm finding out about it from…from you. No offense." She said the last part quickly, and with an extra pinch between her thin furrowed brows.

"None taken," he replied.

Anisa grabbed the back of one of the office chairs lined against the conference table, her fingers denting the dark leather. "I—I'm speechless, really. How could he?" She laughed hollowly.

"Why am I even surprised? Did you know that I had no idea he'd gotten married two months ago?

"Yeah," she continued. "Far more shocking, right? My brother—my *only* sibling—gets married, and I'm learning of it from our Adeero Sharmarke. But that's because he wanted to let me know the good news that Ara had married his daughter, and we're technically family now."

Nasser clenched his fists in disbelief. How could Ara do that to her? Not speaking to her was one thing, but totally isolating a family member from such happy news was an unusual cruelty. He didn't need to know Anisa all that well to understand she didn't deserve such treatment.

After everything he'd heard, her angry display made sense. Naturally, Nasser expected for her to continue to vent. He certainly believed she was entitled to her bitter emotions.

But just as quickly as she'd gotten incensed, Anisa's fury vanished.

She pulled out one of the chairs at the conference table and dropped into it with a long-suffering sigh.

"I don't even know why I bother." Her shoulders slumped, and the last of the fire in her extinguished. Staring blankly in front of her, she said, "I'm not sure if Ara told you, but our parents died in a boating accident. Since their deaths, a lot in our lives has changed. I was young, and

Ara stepped up to take care of me, even though he was only eighteen himself.

"Because of it, I keep thinking that he's my brother, and that I owe it to our parents to try." She paused, taking a breath before she added, "But it's hard to be kind and understanding when he keeps pushing me away and locking me out."

Anisa bowed her head and wrapped her arms around her middle. In the silence that followed, Nasser considered leaving her to her grief. But as he started moving, his feet carried him to her rather than away from her. Before he knew it, he had grabbed the chair beside her.

Looking at Anisa, he saw himself.

They'd both lost family members, and their trauma had affected their relationships with other family. Anisa with her brother, Nasser with his mother and father. And he'd just discovered another shared attribute: Anisa believed her parents to have been killed in a tragic accident, and similarly Nasser's parents didn't know the truth of how their eldest son died. They thought Nuruddin's death had been accidental and were only ever grateful that Nasser had survived the protest rally that took his brother's life.

He hadn't corrected his parents, sparing them the pain of the reality that Nuruddin had been murdered.

"Are you close with your family?" she asked and looked over at him.

The small, sad smile on her face gripped his heart more tightly than he was prepared for. Perhaps that was why he indulged her with a response when he often avoided talking about his family. "It's just my parents, and no, I'm not in contact with them as much I probably should be."

"Is it because of your brother?"

Nasser tensed every muscle, his confusion clearing quickly once he recalled that *he* had been the one to tell her about Nuruddin. Back in the Avenue of the Baobabs, he'd gazed up at the stars and had thought of how his brother had often loved pointing out the different constellations. Then Nasser had let it slip. Though he hadn't gone into detail and hadn't even told her Nuruddin's name, he'd spoken of his brother in the past tense.

And that was enough for her to piece together that Nuruddin wasn't alive.

If he weren't so worried about where their conversation was headed, he would have applauded her deductive reasoning.

"I'm being nosy, sorry," Anisa said. "Feel free to ignore me."

He should have taken her up on the offer, but instead his mouth opened, and Nasser did the last thing he expected. He answered her.

"My brother's death is a factor, yes. It was hard on my family." Far harder because Nuruddin shouldn't have died.

He wouldn't have if cold-blooded killers hadn't taken his life.

Beneath the conference table, Nasser balled his fists, and as he often did when he considered his brother's senseless death, he quietly swore that he'd avenge Nuruddin.

Somehow, some way—

And with Ara's help, he would find those responsible of Nuruddin's murder and mete out justice.

Nasser wasn't sure how long he was gripped by his feverish thirst for vengeance, only that by the time he shook off his vindictive line of thinking, Anisa was on her feet and looking down at him, her eyes large and filled with sorrow for them both.

"I understand how you feel far better than I wish I did," she whispered.

They seemed to have something else in common, because he wished for the exact same thing.

Anisa wouldn't have ever thought depression was contagious, but it had to be. How else could she explain why Nasser looked as unhappy as she felt through the duration of their flight aboard his private jet?

As miserable as she was, she wouldn't have ever vented to him about Ara if she'd known that he'd end up suffering for it too.

I reminded him of his brother, so why wouldn't he be unhappy?

She should have known not to ask about his family, especially since she understood what it felt like to lose someone.

The worst part was that airing out her turmoil hadn't turned her mood for the better.

And now, on top of her misery, guilt lumped in her throat, making every breath harder.

It hadn't gotten easier when they landed in Nosy Be and Nasser arranged a transport from the island airport to a five-star luxury resort. He didn't take credit for it either, but she knew it was him, and it only made her heart sting that much more from the humiliation.

Here he was, treating them so kindly, and all she'd done was dump her problems onto him.

He must now be wishing that he never took me on as a job.

She hoped that the change in scenery would uplift her spirits, but the emerald-green waters, blue skies and endless white beaches pinged off the cloud of doom that trailed her.

Working was the last thing she wanted to do, but once the crew were settled, filming resumed on a new schedule shortly after.

As trying as her job could be, Anisa did like the creative energy on set and the sense of accomplishment at the end of a long workday. It was the upside to what she did. But today she couldn't even rely on that. After dragging herself through work, she dropped into her bed at the end of the day, which at that point was past midnight, and closed her eyes and nodded off.

It felt like only a few seconds later when Anisa's eyes ripped open, her ears flooded by the harsh, grating sound of heavy breathing. Her own, she realized in surprise. She pushed to a sitting position, the collar of her blouse drenched in sweat and the comforter rumpled beneath her. The air-conditioning was off. It explained why she was soaked, but she couldn't as easily settle the matter of her thundering heart.

She hadn't had a night terror in years.

And since she was out of practice, Anisa drew a blank on how to handle her panicked state. Her narrowed gaze darted around her darkened resort room, and her skin itched with her sudden un-ease. It was the scene of her nightmare. But was it her imagination, or did it seem like the space was getting smaller?

She gulped and scurried out of bed.

Before the walls could fully close on her, Anisa fled from her room—*and* narrowly avoided colliding with Nasser. She needn't have asked what he was doing outside her room.

Too bad he can't protect me from bad dreams.

He took one look at her and stepped aside, letting her pass without a word but falling in behind her.

With Nasser as her shadow, Anisa trudged through quiet, well-lit corridors and across the many wooden bridges that connected the different buildings comprising the expansive resort. They didn't run into anyone except a couple of staff members who gave them polite smiles on passing.

Walking over one of those bridges, she slowed and faced the cool ocean breeze wafting from the beach and the silver moon hanging in the sky.

Even in the dark, Nosy Be was idyllic.

Closing her eyes, she tipped her overheated face to the air and breathed slowly. Though the sweat slicking her body and dampening her hair under her hijab was cooling, Anisa still buzzed from the adrenaline rush she hadn't asked for. Her hands seemed to have been hit worst, the trembling in them forcing her to grip the wood railing of the bridge to ground herself.

"Before you ask, it was only a nightmare." She looked over at him, confirming that he was staring at her intently.

"Is that common?" he asked.

Those were the first words they'd traded since their last conversation on his plane. Riddled by guilt for making him think of his deceased brother, Anisa had avoided Nasser, mostly because she didn't know what to say to him.

Unable to evade him now, she nodded slowly and said, "Ever since my parents' death, I've had some variant of a similar dream. But I haven't had it in a while. The only thing that helped back then was teaching myself to dream lucidly. That is, control my dreams."

"Does controlling your dreams no longer help?"

"It always used to. But this…this dream was different."

"How so?"

She flattened her palms against the wood railing. "I couldn't wake up. No matter what I did, I was just stuck in there." Nasser hadn't asked her to go into detail, but now that she was talking, she couldn't stop replaying the vivid sensations the dream imprinted on her. "I'm floating on my back in the middle of the ocean, the sun on my face, and the weightlessness is so relaxing I almost never want to leave. Someone keeps calling my name. Over and over, like they're warning me."

Even now she could hear the echo of her name in the recesses of her mind.

Shaking her head clearer, she continued, "The next thing I know, a motorboat's heading right for me, and I can't move a muscle. Even though my eyes are closed, I somehow know that the driver wants to run me over with the boat."

"Earlier you were telling me about your parents. Perhaps that's why you had the dream," Nasser suggested.

It was a sensible thought, but Anisa knew that wasn't why she was suddenly dreaming of boats.

"Actually, I… I was on the boat with my parents."

She looked up when the quiet had stretched on long enough. Nasser hadn't moved from where he stood facing her, his elbow perched on the wood railing. In the dim lighting, his eyes were as black as the ocean spread before them, but the ocean wasn't weighing what she'd just said, whereas Nasser seemed clearly to be processing her words.

Finally, after another lengthy pause, he said, "Ara did mention how your parents died. He never told me you were there."

"He doesn't like talking about it, and I think it's because he might have lost me too. But that could also just be my wishful thinking that he cares about me." She flashed a tremulous smile and looked away. "I wonder if it's because I'm closer to home than I've been in a long while. Maybe that explains why I'm dreaming of murderous boats and thinking of Ara and my parents more lately."

When a new quiet settled over them, Anisa didn't allow it to stretch as long as before.

"I did it again, didn't I?" she murmured with a grimace. She'd regretted piling her problems onto Nasser once, and now here she was repeating her mistake.

It's just easy to talk to him.

Shocking, really, considering that Anisa didn't want him hanging around. At least, she hadn't…

That's changed now, hasn't it?

Anisa had to admit that she wasn't opposed to his company any longer. Nasser certainly wasn't the person she'd imagined when they had first met. Sure, he still seemed to prefer controlling the situation, and he reminded her of Ara in that way—but unlike her brother, Nasser listened to her rather than shutting her down. He also stuck by her side even though she had tried to push him away. And *yes*, he might have just been doing his job, yet Anisa couldn't help appreciating his iron-willed commitment to protect her.

Which was why she had to tell him, "Listen. I get you're just trying to do your job, and I can't fault you for that. Even though I didn't ask for any of this, I think I owe you an apology. So, I'm sorry."

He sighed, his chest rising and falling from the force of it.

She looked up at him. "For what it's worth, I won't make these last couple days of your job more difficult."

Nasser's lips kicked up at the corners. He hadn't said much since he'd followed her, and Anisa didn't need him to, understanding him perfectly.

Still, he said, "For what it's worth, I appreciate it."

CHAPTER SEVEN

"THAT'S A WRAP!"

The call from the assistant director was met
by a chorus of cheers, laughter and loud clap-
ping. Anisa giggled when Darya hugged her and
jumped up and down with her in place. They only
stopped after Lucas joined them, throwing his
arms around them both and interrupting their private celebration.

"Ew! Lucas, no," Darya laughed and pushed him
back.

He conceded and stepped back but tossed up
his hands. "What? Can't blame me for trying
when I thought I saw room to squeeze in between
you pretty women." He winked, laughingly dodg-
ing Darya's attempt to swat at him.

Anisa rolled her eyes at Lucas's stunt, but her
celebratory mood couldn't be quashed.

After another two days in Nosy Be, two days that
Anisa felt every hour of by the time she crawled
under her bedcovers at the end of the workday,
their crew and cast had officially wrapped film-

ing. Which meant that in less than twenty-four hours, they would be flying out of Madagascar and heading for home in Canada.

Anisa expected to be happier about that news. She was not as elated as she imagined she should be.

And she wasn't the only one who noticed.

"It feels so good to be free!" Darya exclaimed with a stretch of her arms. She paused and pushed her face in closer to Anisa's. "Or…maybe not. Is there a reason you look like you'd rather be working another fourteen-hour shift?"

Anisa gave a snort at that. If there was one thing she wouldn't miss, it was the work hours that stretched from dawn until well past dusk.

"Seriously, what's up?" Darya took her by the arm and steered her away from the ruckus their jubilant crew members were making.

Everyone was chatting loudly and more freely as they deconstructed and cleared the area of lighting and sound equipment, and sets and props were packed and stored for their long journey home.

Anisa knew she and Darya should be helping, but now that her friend had noticed her mood, she couldn't think of anything else.

"It's not that I'm unhappy. I'm more than ready to go home." She was due a break before her next gig started, whatever that was and wherever it took her. "It's just that I feel *off*. Like my brain's too tired to fully comprehend that we're done."

Darya nodded sympathetically, only to look around Anisa and narrow her eyes.

"He wouldn't happen to be the problem, would he?"

Anisa glanced over her shoulder to see what she meant and noticed Nasser entering the area. He had stepped away near the end of shooting with a phone glued to his ear. It was the first time in a while that he'd been away from her side during her waking hours. Strangely, it had worried her a bit when he had walked out of sight. After his call stretched to half an hour, she didn't know what to think.

Grinning, Darya clucked. "I guess now we know what's been bothering you."

"I don't understand what you mean," Anisa said evasively. All the while, her face felt like she had placed it near a furnace. And her cheeks only grew hotter when Nasser's voice sounded from behind her.

"Bonjour."

His French greeting, rumbled in his smooth, deep timbre, raised the fine hairs on her arms and inspired a little skitter of thrill through her.

"Bonjour," she replied breathily. Anisa felt the silly smile on her face, but she was powerless to stop it. If Darya hadn't cleared her throat, she

might have stood there basking in Nasser's un-divided attention for the remainder of the day.

"Are you finished working?" Nasser asked.

"Yeah, we just filmed the last scene."

"Which means we have the whole day to our-selves," Darya added with a teasing nudge to Anisa from behind.

Darya's push brought Anisa that much closer to Nasser. So close she couldn't find air to breathe that wasn't perfumed by his aromatic cologne. Flustered, she tipped her head further back and stared helplessly up at him.

Unfazed by Darya's humor, he gave her friend the curtest of nods. "Then if you don't mind, would you join me for lunch?"

She got the feeling from the way Nasser asked and looked at her—*and only her*—that the invi-tation had initially been meant for her alone. Yet the fact that he didn't wish Darya to feel left out had raised his esteem that much higher for her.

Anisa didn't get the chance to reply immedi-ately. Lucas had come jogging back. Before she and Darya could go on the defensive, he held up his hands to show he had none of his usual las-civious intent. "Easy. I was just wondering if you two are down to go out with everyone and prop-erly celebrate."

"Why not?" Darya didn't even push Lucas off when he dropped his arm over her shoulders with a wide grin.

"Are you in, Anisa?" he asked her, pinning her with a puppy dog look. "It won't feel the same if you're not there."

Anisa stood frozen in indecision. She looked forward to the gatherings at the end of a wrap. But she was certain this time she wasn't bound for their film wrap party but something else.

Someone else, she thought, looking at Nasser.

"Earth to Anisa—are you in there?" Lucas called.

Anisa startled back when Lucas then reached between her and Nasser and snapped his fingers in front of her face.

Nasser shot out his hand and ensnared Lucas's wrist. Everything after that happened in a blur, Nasser's movements so fast and fluid that Anisa blinked in shock by the end. One second Lucas had been snapping his fingers to grab her attention. The next, Nasser had him subdued with his arm pinned in a painful position behind his back.

"Hey, man, let go!" Lucas tried to shake Nasser off him, whining in pain when he couldn't free himself.

Nasser responded by raising Lucas's wrist higher up between his shoulder blades.

That had Lucas shouting for mercy.

"Mind your behavior," Nasser warned before releasing him.

Lucas cradled his arm and, giving Nasser a wide berth, grumbled, "That wasn't cool."

"Let's go." Darya hauled him off, careful to pull the arm that hadn't been pinned by Nasser.

Anisa watched them go, feeling awful for Lucas, but also curious about where Nasser learned self-defensive tactics. "Lucas can be goofy, but he's harmless."

"If he were truly harmless, he wouldn't have touched you."

"But he didn't," she retorted, baffled.

Nasser seemed to believe he had though. A tic in his lower jaw revealed as much. "Before, in Antananarivo, he put his arm around you."

Anisa racked her brain for the memory, and when it clicked, she laughed. "Lake Anosy! I forgot he did that. Like I said, he's handsy but harmless."

Nasser's face hardened to her laughter.

Seeing that he didn't appreciate her humor leeched at her cheery spirits. Though she hadn't wanted to think it, a niggling doubt hatched in her mind. It came with sirens and warning bells, and it cautioned that he wanted to control her. Why else was he acting with such overprotectiveness? It would make sense that her brother would hire a man to protect her who thought like him.

He's no different than Ara, the doubt hissed at her. *He's just trying to find a way to control you.*

Then another part of her cried, *But he saved me! Listened to me! He cares...and how could someone who cares like that want to hurt me by controlling me?*

Anisa didn't know what to think.

"You do believe me when I say that Lucas means me no harm. And that if he did, *if* he really was bothering me, I could handle it myself."

Nasser palmed the lower half of his face, his eyes inscrutable even in the bright light of day.

"Because if you don't, then I think it might be better if you just leave now."

His eyes briefly widened before his brows swooped down and his facial expression intensified in broodiness. For a second, she really thought he would leave, but then he flared his nostrils and gave her a jerky nod.

Quietly she breathed easier, masking just how invested she'd been in him responding favorably.

And she hadn't expected any more from him, happy enough that he hadn't tried to diminish her in an argument. So it was to her profound astonishment that he looked her in the eye and apologized.

"I shouldn't have interfered with your…coworker. It won't happen again."

"That's fine," she said quickly and meekly, surprised that he'd done that much. And she'd thought he was like her brother?

Pfft. Ara would never *apologize to me.*

It was sad, but considering her brother rarely

conceded that he was wrong, she was inclined to believe it to be true.

But Nasser was different.

Her heart thumping a lot faster now and her smile brightening, Anisa floated on a cloud once more, her happiness restored.

Nasser didn't see any of the changes in her. He nudged that steely chin of his at her boisterous coworkers and said, "You're free to go with your friends. I won't take offense if you do."

"I know that."

But when she didn't move, she figured they both understood what her choice was.

"Are you certain?" Nasser asked.

Was she? She could go with her friends, and she didn't doubt that she would like spending the day with them, but Anisa knew in her heart she wouldn't fully be present. The last thing she dreamed of doing was lowering everyone else's joyous mood.

So, with a certainty that slotted in perfectly with her desires, she bobbed her head. "I'm positive."

It wasn't the first time Anisa picked Nasser over her friends. And yet every time, a sense of wonder overcame him.

She chose me.

Not because she had been compelled to, but of her own volition.

He didn't know what he'd done to deserve her attention.

Sure, Nasser had wanted this very outcome. Without a doubt it simplified his job of guarding her, but when all was said and done, he hadn't cared about that as much as he thought he did. Because it was the furthest thing from his mind after she had accepted his lunch invitation.

And it was even further when they finished their meal and Nasser suggested, "There's a lemur park close by, if you would like to walk off the food."

"Are you saying I overate?" she quipped.

Nasser began shaking his head before stopping at the sight of Anisa's mischievous smile. A chuckle burst out of him, low and rumbling, catching him by surprise.

"You should laugh more," she said softly.

His humor ebbed when Anisa's stare captivated him into silence.

She really is a vision.

It was not the first time her beauty bewitched him, and he figured between now and when she boarded her flight for her home tomorrow, it wouldn't be the last.

Rather than fight it, he basked in her loveliness. The sunlight painted a red flush over her beautiful brown skin, added a sparkle to her glossy lips, and forced her eyes to become more squinty from the brightness of the world as she tilted her head up to him. But in the light of day, she looked ready to take on the world in her blush-pink hijab, long-sleeved untucked blouse with an eyelet collar, and high-rise jeans. He hadn't seen her wearing jewelry yet, but today she had on a pair of rose-shaped earrings, the pink in the simple accessory pairing with her headscarf.

She looked good in anything, but there was something in that moment, with her gazing up at him, a soft smile that was meant for him lighting up her face and making his heart do somersaults in his chest. Nasser knew he wouldn't forget it for as long as he lived.

I won't forget her.

It was a dangerous thought, considering she would be leaving soon and he had her brother to answer to. Besides, he had no interest in a relationship and wouldn't curse her with one with him.

They weren't destined for anything more.

And it's better that way.

After Anisa stopped by her room in the resort for a baseball cap and a water bottle, they struck out for their afternoon adventure. The lemur park was a short taxi drive away.

Nasser hadn't planned for it, so he didn't have a rental car prepared as he had on the mainland, but Anisa hadn't minded the canary-yellow tuk-tuk that ferried them to the park. She happily sat through the ride, her eyes glued to the natural landscape of the island and the small, quaint villages they passed through on the quick drive to their destination.

Like everything about this job and even Anisa herself, the trek through the jungle-like park was an experience carved in his long-term memory bank. Mostly because he'd stepped on animal leavings several times, and with thousand-dollar sneakers, no less. He could already envision himself scrubbing the soles, and it wasn't an image he relished.

But Anisa's little cries of joy made up for his despair.

She thrilled at the sight of the lemurs leaping from the tree branches. Once she discovered that the park allowed guests to feed ripened bananas to the overly friendly lemurs, she stood by a low-hanging branch and held a banana over her shoulder, her eyes rounding in delight when a lemur alighted on her shoulder. Anisa giggled as the nimble, long-tailed creature nibbled the piece of banana from her fingertips. No sooner had she finished than she begged him to try.

That was how Nasser ended up with a lemur on him. He had to admit, he could see the appeal when the lemur dug its five-fingered paws into his shoulder, and once it found a good place to perch, it shoved its small, dark face with large round eyes into Nasser's. As he fed the animal, Nasser felt his worries disappear.

An inner peace settled over him for a while, and he embraced it all too readily.

He might have stayed in that mental state for a while longer, but he looked over at Anisa just as she snapped a photo of him with her phone, the flash temporarily blinding him sending the lemur leaping off him and back safely on the tree branch he stood below.

But not before a wetness on his shoulder became apparent. In horror, Nasser realized he didn't only have crap staining his shoes anymore.

"I'm sorry!"

Anisa dabbed a napkin at the stain on his shoulder. She rubbed harder, discouraged when her efforts only made the stain that much bigger. A noise of frustration rose up from the back of her throat, and he must have heard it, because he gently grasped her wrist and drew it down from his big, hard shoulder.

He gave her a squeeze and stilled her attempt to salvage his shirt.

Not for the first time, she apologized profusely.

Nasser shook his head. "It's not your fault. I should have known better."

"But I was the one that pushed you to feed the lemur."

"I didn't refuse, did I?" When she tried to argue, he stood, offered his hand and helped her to her feet. "Had I not wanted to do it, I would've said no. No one holds the blame but me." With a final squeeze of her hand, he released her and found a trash can to dump the soiled napkins in.

Even though his logic was sound, Anisa carried her guilt with her until they came across the park's gift shop and an idea struck her.

A few minutes later, she passed him a plastic bag. In it was a forest-green T-shirt with a large print of the island of Nosy Be.

"It's not much, but I couldn't just let you walk around like that."

Nasser studied the shirt with a curious look. She could have called it gratitude, but his face returned to its impassive state as he left her to find a restroom to change in. She waited for him on pins and needles, worried that she might have chosen the wrong size shirt.

When he finally returned, Anisa almost missed sight of him as he walked right up to her. The shirt molded to his chest and arms perfectly.

Too perfectly.

She was ogling him openly, knew it and was helpless to stop herself.

He raised a brow. "Have I worn it the wrong way?"

Shaking her head, Anisa licked her dry lips and willed her heart rate to slow its wildly drumming tempo.

"I think…"

I think my crush on you is becoming an issue.

"I could use a refreshment."

Several minutes later, with cool lemonade in hand, Anisa and Nasser were strolling down one of the footpaths of the lemur reserve and outdoor park. She was still having a hard time regulating her body temperature around him, but Anisa wasn't feeling as feverish as she had been earlier. And even though silence hung over them, it was peaceful for once.

She sighed happily, closing her eyes and absorbing her surroundings. It was just the thing she needed after finishing up with work. Just the moment to clear her head of Ara, their lack of a relationship, her worry for him…

And Nasser.

Suddenly, the distinct sound of ice being crushed rose above the noise of the small park animals skittering through the thick green tropical foliage and the chatter of tourists milling about.

Anisa opened her eyes and smiled. "Are you munching on an ice cube?"

He stopped chewing the instant she asked, appearing adorably abashed.

"Old habit," he mumbled once he swallowed and cleared his mouth of the evidence.

"Darya chews on ice, too. She usually does it when she's nervous." Anisa was only teasing when she asked, "You're not nervous, are you?"

"Not nervous. Confused."

She hadn't expected his response and wasn't

prepared when he stared down at her with an intensity that left her quietly breathless.

"Why did you choose to come with me and not go along with your friends?"

Anisa shook her head slowly with a shrug. "Truthfully? I don't know. But I guess you looked like you could use the excitement of company more."

It was Nasser's turn to be surprised.

"You don't look like the type that has fun," she explained, chuckling. "I mean, I get that you're working right now, guarding me and all, but how do you unwind after work?"

His brow creased. "My career choice doesn't spare much room for 'fun,' not when my clients are typically at the most vulnerable points of their lives."

Undaunted by his change of expression, Anisa said, "Okay, I'll give you that. And yet you've only proven my point that you could use some more downtime." She spied a bench up ahead on their path and steered him to it. Then, dropping to the seat, she patted the space beside her. "A little R & R never hurt anyone."

"R & R?"

She smiled. "Rest and relaxation."

"I see. And what exactly do you do for…downtime?"

Smiling more sheepishly, she admitted, "I try to squeeze in some rest between jobs, but sometimes it doesn't always work. Lately I've been picking up more gigs to make ends meet, since rent isn't going to pay itself." She frowned then, thinking about what she'd rather be doing for a living, her screenwriting, but knowing that it wasn't paying her bills right now. "I'll probably take a few days off after I fly out tomorrow, let the jet lag run its course, and then hop back into another job. Only maybe this time it won't be a sad romance. I don't think I could handle another tear-jerker."

"Is that what you and your crew were filming? A romance?"

"Yeah," she said. "Two star-crossed lovers, one of them dying, and the other one going through a contentious divorce, fated to reunite on a tour of Madagascar. At least that's the short, logline version."

"Are those the kind of stories you want to write?"

"Maybe one day, but it'd have to be less tragic. Who wants to cry when they're watching people fall in love?" Anisa blew a long sigh. "Until then, PA gigs are all I got."

"So what you're saying is that you could use this R & R too," he drawled.

Anisa laughed and swatted his arm—or she aimed to, missing and landing on his chest instead. Her laughter cut off abruptly on a breathy hitch, her eyes widening and jaw slackening.

Time seemed to slow as Nasser looked down to her hand lying flat and unmoving against his pec. He raised his head just as unhurriedly, his gaze finding hers, and his unaffected expression making it hard for her to tell what he was thinking. Despite that, desire unspooled anew in her, its tendrils winding around her every nerve, fiber, muscle, and bone, before finally ensnaring her heart.

Pulling back as though she'd scalded her palm, she rubbed her hands together and, in a hurry to deflect from her social gaffe, stammered, "Wh-what were we talking about?"

"Having fun," he said, his voice low and deliciously gruff.

"Right," she croaked nervously. *"Fun."*

I'm soft for her.

In and of itself, that revelation was innocuous. And unless he chose to pursue it, *pursue her,* his attraction for her and any feelings of attachment would pose no problem for them. He was optimistic that he could control himself. But that optimism faltered when she stopped to pull her shoes and socks off, bared her slim brown ankles and wriggled cute toes before she treaded the beach barefoot. Nasser pulled a long, audible swallow, the sweat on his brow having less to do with the heat wafting off the beach sands.

Anisa drew her baseball cap off her head to

fan her face. Her hijab still covered her hair, but now he could see her face more clearly, see the way her eyes slanted up at him coyly.

"Where did you learn what you did to Lucas?" She pretzeled her arms in a crude mime of how he'd subdued her handsy coworker.

"The army." He replied without thinking, her beautiful face the only thing he could focus on until he heard himself speak. He watched the way her eyes rounded and her lips parted with her surprise.

"You were in the military."

"Years ago, yes."

Nasser didn't like to speak of it, mostly because it made him think of what he'd done to end up an instrument of the army.

"So, why the military?"

Nasser could tell her the truth: he'd been given an ultimatum to rot in jail for crimes he was being accused of perpetrating, or save himself and serve the government that was trying to silence him.

And this only after he had been locked up for one horrendously long week and given a taste of criminal sanction.

His choice after that was obvious. Not only hadn't he wanted to spend another second in that overcrowded cell with *real* convicts who had committed *real* crimes, but for his parents' sake, he wished to spare them the humiliation on top of the sorrow of losing Nuruddin. They'd lost one son; Nasser hadn't wanted them to mourn another.

But most of all, he'd been a scared young boy, barely fifteen and freshly grieving his brother's murder.

When the timeline flashed in front of him, he gritted his teeth and abandoned telling her the whole truth.

What would it serve to reopen old wounds?

"I joined the military for my family." Spying Anisa's brows fly up in response, he explained, "My older brother had been in the military, and he was an outstanding officer." Nuruddin had been young, bright, and eager to serve his country. "He loved what he did, and he was studying to be a politician someday."

"I'm guessing you two were close," Anisa said, her kind voice in one way soothing the pain in his heart that arose whenever he mentioned his brother, but in another way, her sweetness made it all the harder because he didn't want her pity.

"We were very close." He aimed his stare ahead, at the point where the alien green jungle of the island bordered the white smoothness of its shore. Risking any chance of seeing the all-too-familiar look of distress on Anisa was not something he wanted to do, not when he knew it would unlock the emotions restlessly rattling within him. Free them for the first time in years—

And not since Nuruddin's death had he cried.

He had no idea what chaos his long-bottled-up feelings would unleash. So he thought better of looking at her while he continued, for both their sakes.

"After he died, I decided to go into the military. My brother's salary wouldn't be discontinued, and I could help my parents.

"It wasn't easy, but my time there brought its lessons and growth, and I'm not sure if I would change my experience," he lied.

His military life had been one long tirade of verbal abuse from his superiors and grueling training regimes. While honing his body and polishing his war skills, they'd also beaten out any emotional vulnerability. He'd quickly learned sharing his thoughts and feelings was the surest way to punishment and gave him the furthest chance of surviving his ordeal.

And yet, though his time in the military hadn't been kinder than prison, Nasser had more freedom than he would have from behind prison bars. More importantly, without his military background, he wouldn't have discovered the private security sector.

"After nearly a decade in the military, I was discharged honorably and found work in private security. I loved the job, and eventually realized I could begin my own company doing the same work. That was six years ago," he said with a small smile full of self-pride. He'd been young when he became his own boss and when, for the first time in his life, he felt in control of his own destiny.

"I'm glad something good came of it then, but I'm still sorry for your personal loss."

Anisa's kindness nearly pried the truth from him. He pressed his lips together, forcing his secrets back in. Aside from founding his company, nothing truly good had happened to him since Nuruddin passed away. Losing his brother upended Nasser's whole life. Before Nuruddin's death, he used to laugh freely, voice his opinions and talk of his emotions, but like his brother, that was taken from him.

Gleaming fiery gold above the calm ocean waters, the sun dipped lower toward the horizon, the sky changing from clearest blue to vibrant pinks and purples.

They grabbed another tuk-tuk back into town, where Anisa answered an alert from her phone and reported that her coworkers were at a local jazz festival. The festivities weren't hard to spot when they poured from the homes and buildings into the town streets. People were dancing to the live music, families strolled among the many vendors displaying their wares, and couples held fast onto each other through overexuberant crowds.

Nasser found the noise in Nosy Be to be peaceful, and just the balm he needed to reset his restless heart and mind.

"Darya messaged that they were over by the main stage indoors." Anisa looked up from her phone and around, her face scrunching in puzzlement. "But I don't see any directions."

The mention of her friends wasn't the most appealing thought after a day greedily spent with her alone, but Nasser helped her by asking a friendly-faced shopkeeper for the way to the main event. Once he had what he needed, he purchased an item in gratitude and relayed what was said to Anisa. Then they were off in search of her coworkers.

"What did you buy?" Anisa wondered as they were walking.

"Something that was needed."

Aside from casting him the most curious of looks, Anisa quietly let his cryptic response stand.

The smile playing at his lips froze as the loudest crack erupted from the streets somewhere behind them. The startling noise rose above the din of the crowds and awakened his adrenaline. Running purely in fight-or-flight mode, Nasser herded Anisa down a narrow alley. There, sandwiched by two squat buildings, he secured her against him, his back caging her behind him, his body between her and whatever danger was close by.

Nasser slowed his breathing, knowing that he couldn't lose his head when the muscles in his arms and legs were taut for action. The feel of her hand latching onto the back of his gift shop

T-shirt reminded him that Anisa was relying on him. Even though she'd been fighting this protection detail from the start, her fear was palpable now.

"What's wrong?" she asked hoarsely, her nails pinching at his flesh as the thin material of his shirt yielded to her powerful, fear-induced grip.

"I'm not sure," he reported back, but he wasn't going to stand there and wait for any threat to find them first.

Peeking out of the alley, Nasser faced a scene of normalcy. People were chatting and laughing, and some were still dancing in the streets to the bumping beats of jazz strumming out of stereos. He relaxed once there weren't other signs of peril.

A group of gangly-limbed teenagers streaked past, one of the kids holding a string of firecrackers.

"A firecracker," she breathed, her eyes rolling back in relief and her hand falling away from his shirt. "I thought…"

She didn't need to finish what she was saying. Because he had been thinking the exact same thing.

As relieved as he was that it was merely firecrackers that raised the alarm, he was embarrassed for overreacting and frightening her for no reason.

"I should have figured it was fireworks," he grumbled down at her.

"Festivals and fireworks do go hand in hand,"

she agreed softly before angling her head back to rest on the stone wall behind her. Trapped between him and that wall at her back, Anisa had nowhere to go, unless she sidled away from him. Judging by the way she leaned back, she was in no hurry to leave.

Not even when a giggling young man and woman, their arms wrapped around each other, lips locked passionately, tumbled into the mouth of the alley. Sensing them, they came up for air and stopped a few feet shy of them. They then laughed as if they thought it the funniest coincidence that another couple would have considered the alley for the same purposes.

The young lovey-dovey couple scurried away together after that, vanishing as quickly as they had come.

Their precarious position dawned on Nasser then.

He only imagined what it must have appeared they were doing. With Anisa looking up at him, her lips soft and glistening, her skin dewy from their action-packed day, and her body so close to his that he could see the pulse at the base of her neck. And with him leaning as close to her as possible without actually touching her, his arms held tensely at his sides and thumbs pressed to the seams of his pants as though he were standing at attention for an army drill. It was the only thing he could do to stop himself from touching

her. Cupping her cheek and holding her head still
for when he claimed her sweet-looking mouth.

A kiss.

He wanted it so desperately that his muscles
strained and his body vibrated from denying himself.

And what trouble could one little buss on the
mouth cause them?

Besides everything?

Nasser pressed a hand against the wall by her
head. Using his other hand, he cradled her chin
with his thumb and forefinger and turned her face
up to him even more.

"Anisa."

He said her name with low, guttural intent. If he
didn't have the power to stop himself, he needed
her to do it. Because right then, he didn't care
that she was forbidden to him, or that her brother
might do him serious damage for touching her,
and he wasn't of the mind to consider how she
might misconstrue his actions. All that mattered
to him was satisfying this driving, damning need
for her.

Stop me, he begged her silently.

He nearly roared in frustration when she didn't.
"Nasser," she keened, her back arching up off
the wall, the space between their bodies close to
sealed.

His brain warned that they shouldn't, but his
heart…?

His heart was about ready to fly out of his chest and into her hands, where it would be putty for her to mold into whatever shape she deemed fit.

This was going to happen.

He would throw caution away and kiss her, hard and fast—or possibly soft and slow. He only knew he required it, like he needed the next breath of air.

"Yes," Anisa breathed as his head swooped down, their faces pushing in tantalizingly closer.

His phone ringing saved them both from what would certainly have been a grave slip of judgment.

The caller identified himself as Daniel, the team lead of the security personnel he'd tasked to work on Ara's shipping business. Since Ara first hired the services of Nasser's company ten months ago, Daniel and his capable team had been on the ground at Ara's headquarters in self-declared Somaliland's capital, Hargeisa, and were responsible for updating cyber and physical security, among other things like breach prevention and security training for Ara's staff.

Daniel's call was the last thing he expected, though.

They'd primarily communicated via email, aside from their brief quarterly updates via teleconference. And those calls didn't involve just him and Daniel but the whole company, his board of directors included.

"What is it?" Nasser cut to the chase, his eyes never moving off Anisa.

Daniel didn't prolong the suspense. "It's Mr. Abdullahi—Ara, sir. He's missing."

CHAPTER EIGHT

No! ANISA WANTED to cry out when Nasser hadn't ignored his ringing phone.

She dug her nails into her palms to stop herself from reaching for him. Her body coursed with desire, her chest heaving with her yearning, her every thought replaying the delicious seconds before Nasser was pulled from her. And every second he had the phone glued to his ear was a second more that she burned uselessly for what could have been between them.

But when his searing looks turned to ice, Anisa sensed something was wrong.

Seriously so. What else could explain the steely set to Nasser's jaw? His face was void of emotion, but his hands were clenched and his movements sharp and jerky, his voice curt with the caller.

It sounded as if he knew whoever it was. From the brusque manner of his speech, she would guess that it was someone who worked for him.

She relaxed at the thought that it was a work-related call. He'd told her about his company.

Running a business couldn't be easy, and his attention must be in demand. And it wouldn't be the first time that day he had answered a call. He had been on his phone earlier, while she'd been doing her own work with her film crew. It was possible that the two calls were related to the same issue.

Yeah, that's it. Just a work call. Nothing more.

She was further reassured when Nasser said, "And you've begun protocol measures for this? Good. Yes, keep me updated."

Expecting him to come closer to her, even take her in his arms this time and resume what they'd begun, Anisa was disappointed by his retreat to the alley's opening.

"We're heading back to the resort."

The last lingering threads of her longing sloughed off at his command.

"No," she refused, confused and irritated. "We're supposed to meet with my coworkers. Darya is waiting for me."

"Message her to meet you at the resort."

"Why are you in a rush to head back?" She didn't voice her suspicion any more than that, not wanting to feed the anxiety now scratching and clawing around her insides.

His dreadful scowl wasn't helping allay her unease.

"I will answer your questions in your room at the resort. It would be far more appropriate, trust me."

"*Trust* you?" She stepped closer to him, her

heart jackhammering in her chest. "How can I trust you when all you do is give me orders and expect me to jump? Besides, trust is a two-way street, and you've given me no reason to believe that you'll ever answer any of my questions."

In a gravelly voice, he grumbled, *"Ah vraiment,"* and she didn't need translation because it sounded like he sarcastically challenged what she'd accused him of.

But what set her off was the way he swiped a hand down his face and heaved a sigh replete with exasperation. Like she was a chore he was ready to be rid of at last. Gawking at him, Anisa couldn't believe he was the same person who'd just had her pinned to an alley wall, ready to ravish her seconds before he took the call that had totally shut him down.

She didn't recognize him.

What hurt most was that she'd thought they were getting closer. Felt the signs of mutual interest and attraction from him. After all, he had told her about his brother and his background in the military, and weren't they sure signs that he was opening up to her and letting her in?

I don't think he ever intended to let me in.

"Anisa, please." The fear that was circling her like sharks in chum-infested waters tightened at the plea softening his voice. She might have weakened had he not stepped closer a moment later and said, "This is not the place and time to fight me when all I'm trying to do is protect you."

Freshly incensed, Anisa raised her chin and huffed, "First, I *never* asked for your protection. And, as you already know, I'm not going anywhere. Not until you explain why you're acting so weird suddenly."

Nasser leveled one of his intense stares on her, but other than the usual fluttering in her belly, she was impervious to it. Whether he finally realized it had no effect, or that she wouldn't be budged on this, he sighed heavily again and dipped his chin passively.

"Very well. I would have preferred to do this elsewhere."

"Noted," she rejoined, her sarcasm thick. She normally wouldn't have been so petty, but Anisa couldn't forget how quickly he'd gone from hot to cold on her—or how easily he'd believed she would jump to his command.

"I just spoke with my team lead, who's been stationed with your brother's company in Hargeisa."

So it was exactly what she suspected: Nasser had taken a work call. Yet Anisa wasn't following what her brother had to do with it. She nodded for him to continue.

"He's been working closely with Ara."

Anisa muttered, "I'm not surprised. Ara likes having everything done his way." Her brother wouldn't trust anyone's work unless he was

double- if not *triple*-checking the process and results himself.

"He and I are alike in that way, yes."

Yes. Yes, you two are.

Anisa snapped, "Just tell me what you're not
saying."

"Ara's missing."

Somewhere close to the alley, Anisa heard the
familiar popping of firecrackers go off once more,
followed by an eruption of applause and laughter, but the noise might as well have come down
a long tunnel at her over the sudden shrill ringing in her ears.

"What do you mean he's missing?" she asked
on a croak, her mouth running dry, her head spinning with a flurry of questions.

"It seems your brother has been involved in an
attack, but it's too early to tell whether he was the
intended target."

"Attack?" she gasped.

"From what I understand, your brother hadn't
informed my team that he'd be traveling to Mogadishu. A car bomb detonated outside the hotel he
was staying at, and he hasn't been counted among
the injured living. Or the dead."

The dead.

Those words circled through Anisa's mind until
she shook her head in bewilderment. "A bomb?
In Mogadishu? I don't understand. Why was he
so far south?"

"That's what I intend to find out." But not even Nasser's determined tone and firm expression alleviated her distress at the terrible news.

"He's really missing?" Anisa whispered, her voice breaking. At Nasser's solemn nod, a streak of hot bile surged a fiery trail from her chest up her esophagus and flooded her mouth. She cupped her mouth and gagged, slapping a hand on the cool stone wall of the building to ground her unsteady legs. Squeezing her eyes shut, she cried.

She couldn't wrap her mind around the fact that her brother—the *only* family she had left—was missing. She hadn't spoken to Ara in years, and for what? A childish disagreement.

Allah, please! Don't let him leave me alone.

Her breaths dragged raggedly from her lungs now, like she was drowning.

I know what that's like.

Closing her eyes tighter and biting her lip, she tumbled headfirst into a vision of a crying little girl wading deeper into the ocean, fighting the tide to get to something she wanted so desperately that her body propelled her against the tallest of white waves the ocean could throw at her. Anisa sobbed as she realized she was the little girl, limbs thrashing in the waters, her head dipping under the surface and her lungs filling up with the ocean. She'd never thought she would feel like she was drowning again, but here she was.

Sinking.

Slipping under.

Unable to keep her head above water.

Only now it's not the ocean that's killing me…

It was the reality she might lose her brother that was slowly suffocating her.

The only thing that saved her from going completely under was the recognizable scent of Nasser, his body heat in front of her and his voice calling her back.

"Look at me, Anisa," he urged, panic underlying his voice.

Pitiful whimpering sounded from somewhere in the alley with them… Anisa recognized it was coming from her. Shocked by herself, she opened her eyes slowly, her lids fluttering and her vision swimming with her sorrow. The open concern on Nasser's face blurred anew. She blinked rapidly, feeling more tears splash her cheeks and drip down from her chin. Broken, that was what she was. She felt like a leaking faucet that could never be repaired.

"I'm taking you to the resort. Now." His brusque tone suggested that she'd best not think of arguing with him.

The fight having gone from her, Anisa let him do what he'd wanted from the start. It was easier to allow him to have his way.

Far easier than it was to face a world her brother might not be in anymore. A world where she was left well and truly alone.

* * *

If Anisa were asked how she'd ended up back at her room in the resort, she wouldn't be able to say exactly. The ride from town to their beach-side resort was one big blur. All she knew was that one second she was crying in an alley with Nasser staring down at her in abject concern, and the next he was guiding her into her room, pointing out things she shouldn't trip over rather than touching her. She wasn't too far gone emotionally and mentally to miss noticing that he avoided contact with her. Anisa should've been relieved he was being so kind and gentlemanly, but right then, she could have seriously used a hug.

Knowing there was no chance that Nasser would give that much-needed physical comfort to her, she wrapped her own arms around herself, squeezing until a sense of wholeness came over her.

Still, feeling fragile and staring anxiously at the four walls that now surrounded her, Anisa's gaze landed on the sliding patio doors.

"Careful," he cautioned gently when she bumped the corner of the coffee table on her way out to the patio.

She needed fresh air. Being confined in her resort when her brother was out there somewhere had her skin crawling.

Because now that her head was clearing, and she wasn't drowning from the grief of learning that Ara was missing, Anisa refused to believe that her brother was gone.

He's alive.

She didn't know how she knew, only that her gut and heart wouldn't let go of that strong conviction.

She looked out over the expansive green separating her from the gleaming white beach and deep blue ocean beyond. A breeze waved the drooping branches of the palm trees scattered over the lawn and teased goose bumps from her overheated body. Surrounded by such natural and manmade beauty, but Anisa couldn't dredge up the emotion to care about anything other than the tightly coiled ball of anxiety pressurizing her chest.

She didn't care about her legs hurting from standing there until the sky darkened and the last of the sun's rays faded below the ocean's horizon.

She was barely cognizant of the night ferrying in chillier temperatures, the nip of the breeze slipping under her clothing and wrapping itself around her jittery bones. Or how her stomach clenched and twisted, not only from the omnipresent fear for Ara, but out of simple hunger now.

Anisa even missed the sliding door opening until Nasser spoke to her.

"Anisa, come in. I ordered room service."

Not facing him, she shook her head.

She heard his sigh drift to her, the frustration

in his voice tempered when he said, "You have to eat."

"Why?" she sniped, forcing back a sniffle. "Ara's out there, alone, maybe with no shelter or food."

"You don't know if he's alone."

Anisa turned stiffly to him, her eyes wide and her lips trembling. "If I know my brother, he's probably alone. He's always done everything *alone*. Even when he's surrounded in a room full of people, he's always by himself."

Nasser leaned against the sliding door, filling the doorway but not making a move to cross the threshold. For a moment he just returned her stare with the same blankness she projected, only he wore his poker face far better. She felt the cracks forming in hers.

Feeling an urge to cry swell over her, she sharply whipped her head away and sucked in her lips to trap the sob that would've emerged.

She wished, in a way, that she could be as stoic as Nasser. Then maybe she wouldn't feel misplaced guilt that this was all her fault somehow. Perhaps she could have talked her brother out of whatever he'd done that had gotten him into this mess. She didn't need to know his secrets or Nasser's to sense that they both had something to do with what had happened to Ara.

"Anisa…" Nasser spoke her name quietly, like he was using it to substitute reaching out to her physically. "If you won't eat for yourself, then eat for him. You'll need energy to stay strong until he returns."

Her bottom lip wobbled, his soft voice breaking through her stubborn shell.

"Come in. Eat," he coaxed her, promising, "and I swear that I will do whatever is in my ability to find out what has happened to Ara and track him down."

She lowered her arms and faced him again, her eyes stinging but the tears held at bay for now.

Nasser extended a hand to her. It wasn't the first time he'd done it, but having longed for that form of connection with him since they left the alley after learning of Ara's disappearance, Anisa latched onto it greedily without another word. Staring down at his larger hand engulfing hers, she calmed, not feeling left alone anymore.

"He'll be okay, won't he?"

Nasser kept his emotions locked and guarded from her, but when he jerked his chin in affirmation, she knew that he would do exactly as he vowed and then some. She released the last doubts assailing her and allowed him to ease her back inside, where not only a warm dinner awaited, but the company of a man who in that moment earned the right to be called her protector.

"Merde."

Nasser uttered the curse, not normally resorting to profanity, but also not in the right state of mind to be polite and poised right then. It was taking every ounce of his willpower to maintain his composure around Anisa, knowing that she needed the brave front more than anything else, but also aware that now wasn't the time for him to have a breakdown.

He had calls to make, and a window to make them alone when Anisa started drifting asleep. She'd started yawning after she managed to clean half of her plate. As much as he would have liked her to finish eating, he couldn't entirely blame her for not having an appetite.

It had been hard for Nasser to do much of anything after Nuruddin died. Sleeping, eating, and even taking his spot in the army had fired up his remorse for having lived when Nuruddin hadn't.

No matter what he said, Anisa's concern for Ara would persist until she heard news of him, one way or another.

And now he'd promised to be the bearer of the news—whether it was good or bad. The thought of giving her news she didn't want to hear heaped additional hurdles on the already daunting task of searching for Ara.

He left Anisa where she lay on the sofa, her head on the armrest and her legs drawn up under a white quilt.

Phone pressed to his ear, he stepped outside, closed the sliding door behind himself and took position where Anisa had stood not too long ago.

And there he remained until the blue hour before dawn. Nasser ended what had to be the twentieth call and headed indoors, where he discovered Anisa crying in her sleep.

Pained at the sight of the tears beading out of the corners of her eyes, Nasser crouched beside her and gently shook her awake. He watched as she opened her eyes and blinked blearily up at him, her drowsiness melting away and a look of alarm compressing her brows.

"Is it Ara?" She sat up. "Did you hear from him?"

Nasser had hoped to have some time to gather his thoughts before she woke up, but he'd had time to confirm the news, and he knew it was far more of a torture for Anisa to imagine the worst happening to Ara than it was for him to tell her what he had learned.

"Your brother's been found, and he's alive," he reported, moving from his haunches to a seat on the coffee table in front of her.

She expelled a loud *whoosh* of breath replete with her relief.

"But he's been injured."

Anisa shot up to her feet, her eyes wild with fear.

"He'd been traveling down south, intending to conduct business there." From what Nasser had understood, Ara had briefly left Hargeisa and Somaliland and was pursuing a government contract that would allow him to build a port in Somalia's capital, Mogadishu, that would expand the opportunity for international trade.

Since Ara still owed him the names of the true culprits behind Nuruddin's murder, Nasser presumed that her brother's business travel disguised another motive. But he wouldn't be able to verify it with anyone other than Ara himself.

"He's been admitted to an international hospital in Mogadishu. During emergency surgery—"

"Surgery?" Gasping the word, Anisa swayed in place with her hands pressed to her chest.

In response to her distress, Nasser clenched his fists, but without any real specter to fight, he could do nothing for her but relay the information that would be of most use to her. "Doctors induced a medical coma because of some head trauma, and he's still under from what I understand."

"Coma? He's not conscious."

"I hear the surgery's been successful."

"But what if he…he doesn't…" A shudder rocked her body, her lips pinching together as if the words pained her physically. He knew what she was thinking, knew what she'd been about to say.

What if Ara never wakes up?

And what if his death stole any chance that Nasser might have had at learning the identities of and punishing his brother's killers?

As real as that fear was for him, it was a selfish

thought to entertain when Anisa was mourning her brother's mishap. Shame swiftly blanketed him, and with it guilt that prompted him to comfort her.

"He will," Nasser said.

She bobbed her head heavily, all her movements sluggish, weighed down by her concern for Ara.

Glancing at his dress watch, Nasser frowned at the time.

"Have you finished packing? Your flight is soon, isn't it?"

"My flight?" Anisa raised her head from staring blankly at the floor.

"For Antananarivo." Along with her film crew and the cast, Anisa was flying out of tropical Nosy Be to Madagascar's capital. From there they would be heading back to their homes. The moment she was safely boarded spelled the end of Nasser's protection detail of her.

In a few short hours, there would no longer be a purpose to speak to or see one another.

No reason to stop us from becoming strangers once more.

His gut flexed uncomfortably at that. Not exploring what it could mean, he concentrated on Anisa's pinging phone.

"It's Adeero Sharmarke," she said after observing the screen, her eyes growing saucer-wide again. "Nasser, he's with Ara." She looked to him in shock.

Nasser nodded, his head feeling heavier by the moment. "I know. My team told me. Apparently Ara had taken his wife along to Mogadishu as well."

"He's texting again, asking if I'm coming to Mogadishu."

Nasser's heart thudded, piecing together where she was going with this.

"I can't leave," she said quietly.

Damn.

He hadn't bargained on Ara being injured— and then he hadn't factored in Anisa wanting to stay, though it made perfect sense that she would. Anyone in her place would feel the same.

But where did that leave him and the issue of him protecting her?

She must have read his mind, because Anisa walked away from him into the bedroom. Nasser trailed after her, finding her dropping her suitcase on her bed and opening it, her jerky movements as she stuffed her clothes into her luggage smacking of desperation to be by her brother's side.

"I have to go to him," she announced.

Nasser pinched the bridge of his nose, breathing deeply to generate a calm he wasn't feeling.

"That's not possible."

Anisa whirled on him. "Why? Because you won't allow me."

Yes, he wanted to say, but knowing it would add

oil to the fire blazing in her eyes, he said, "No, because there's nothing you can do for him now."

"He'll want to see me when he wakes. He *should* see me. I'm family. He needs his family right now."

"And he does have family with him. There's his wife and your *adeero*."

"I have to do something!" she cried, pressing her hands over her mouth and bowing her head before dropping down onto the bed by her suitcase, now half-filled and temporarily forgotten.

Nasser reacted on pure instinct, and it drove him to her side.

Sitting by her on the bed, and leaving an appropriate amount of space between them, he slid forward, perched his elbows over his legs and nervously clenched and unclenched his hands. He had stood in front of dour-faced directors from his board, led business panels in front of thousands of professionals, and handled clients from powerful oligarchs to well-heeled politicians. Yet somehow, despite his experiences, he was gripped by the fear that he wouldn't be enough. That he was too inept to offer her the solace she needed.

I have to try, though.

After she'd told him about having survived the accident that took her parents' lives, being terrorized by her nightmares, and now this fear for her brother's well-being, he would be a coward if he ignored her pain. So before he broke out in a sweat, Nasser dispelled the quiet oppressing them in the darkened bedroom.

"Anisa, the best thing you can do for him is take care of yourself. He wouldn't want to see you like this when he wakes and recovers."

She was silent for a long while. He measured the time by the way the room brightened with the first rays of dawn.

Finally, she softly asked, "What if he thinks I don't care?"

Nasser could see why she would imagine that. What with her not having spoken to her brother for years, the fear she voiced was natural. Not for the first time, he silently cursed Ara, swearing that if he had the chance, he'd give him a good dressing-down on Anisa's behalf.

"What if he thinks I've abandoned him?"

"Anisa, if he truly thinks that way about you, then that's more his problem than yours." He sat up, planting his hands on the bed by his thighs and meeting her wary expression. "But from what I have seen, that's not the kind of man your brother is." For all his faults, Ara could be generous. Nasser knew he was quite philanthropic and did what he could to give back. Just like his father, his efforts to expand Somalia and Somaliland's exports and imports were all for the good of the citizens. More international trade would help uplift the economy and generate the funds required for public infrastructure.

Ara was a man of his country and people.

The two men weren't different there. No matter the wealth he attained, Nasser never forgot his roots, his past forming his present and paving the way for his future. That fueled his current quest to avenge Nuruddin.

"Ara wouldn't want you to put yourself in harm's way for him. You can doubt anything else, but that much you shouldn't. It's why he sent me, after all."

He didn't know if he got through to her until she spoke up again.

"What should I do then?" she wondered.

Nasser was more than a little taken aback. Since he'd met Anisa, she had made it a point to do what she wanted, including being open about her emotions. He envied her for being so free with her feelings, but right then, he didn't even mask his befuddlement.

Adding to the rattle in his head, in the space between their bodies, Anisa's pinkie finger brushed the side of his hand atop the bed. He froze, holding still as her finger caressed him again. The simple touch unlocked a fissure of heat that steadily burned in him from that point on.

Speaking around it was difficult, his voice noticeably husky even to his ears. "I'm not sure."

"What would you do in my position?"

What would he do? Nasser struggled to make sense of his thoughts, hyperaware that her hand was still touching his. He finally replied, "I would want to be close by, in case of any change of news."

"So, if I asked you to take me home?"

Again, not hiding his surprise, his brows snapped up. "You wish for me to take you back to Canada?" It wasn't part of the deal with Ara, but if Anisa wanted his company, he wouldn't deny her.

A shake of her head dropped his mood. Aside from his disappointment, he remained confused. He opened his mouth to ask her what she meant, only to snap his jaws together the instant it clicked in his mind.

"You mean…"

He didn't finish the thought as she shyly nodded.

She wanted to go home to Somaliland. Berbera, specifically. He hadn't considered it an option, only knowing that he wouldn't send her to Mogadishu where terrorist attacks, banditry, and other dangers could find her. The quaint coastal city of Berbera wasn't exactly a hotbed of crime. The most he could look forward to was more beaches.

Decision made, he said, "I'll take you home then."

She placed her hand over his in what he supposed was wordless gratitude. It lasted only a moment before she took her hand away, smiled beautifully, pushed onto her feet and resumed gathering her things from her bedroom.

Nasser left her to it, promising he'd meet back

with her once he cleared his own room of his few belongings, and catching himself flexing the hand she'd touched, the heated longing she'd stirred up in him still alive and simmering.

CHAPTER NINE

"THAT CAN'T BE the house." Anisa's jaw slackened at the sight of her childhood home, unable to recognize the exterior even though it was still on the same plot of land overlooking the beach that neighbored it. Ara's changes to their home were significant. The most obvious were the stories he'd added to the original build. She counted a total of three as they approached, the sun glinting off the many windows, forcing her to squint her eyes and roll her window back up. Nasser steered his black truck up the well-paved private drive, the smooth asphalt bringing them much faster to the steel driveway fence gate and the tall stone enclosure barricading the house and its grounds.

The gates rolled open almost on command, and Nasser didn't stop driving until they were past the front line of security measures and rolling into the wide, stone-paved front yard of the home. Before they even stopped, they were surrounded by half a dozen men, earpieces plugged in, moving in unison to canvass all sides of the truck. They would have made for a menacing sight all on their own, but to make matters more distressing, Anisa spied thigh holsters.

She was used to Ara having a couple of body-guards on him, but this level of protection was excessively cautious. Tearing her eyes off the small army of security personnel, Anisa climbed out of the truck, shielded the sunlight from her eyes and peered up. "Is that a terrace on the roof?"

"It is."

Her head whipped to him. "You've been up there?"

"I've had the pleasure of being up there a couple of times. Your brother seems to enjoy the roof-top addition immensely."

Anisa gave it another considering look, and it could've been the shock of seeing all the changes to the home, but she didn't see what the hype was about. She dropped her head and forced her feet forward to the front door. Pulling in a deep breath, she grabbed the handle and pushed her way inside. Expecting the interior to be just as disconcertingly unfamiliar to her, she shielded herself for the reveal.

She breathed easier when everything inside appeared almost as it had when she lived there. Of course the details that were unrecognizable jumped out at her, but it wasn't as alien as she imagined it would be. The entryway was wider and the ceilings higher than she recalled. A skylight washed the light of day over her and brightened up the area. A curved staircase with dark wood treads and a bright white banister wound to the upper floors, and a pretty black birdcage chandelier hung above the stairway, beckoning her with its warm, inviting light.

Anisa took a step off the entrance mat onto the gleaming white-and-black patterned tiles beneath her scuffed-up sneakers. Looking down, she heard the memory of her mother's voice gently scolding her to take her shoes off.

As she pulled off her shoes, Nasser caught up with her. He rolled her luggage in, followed her lead and left his footwear by the entrance, and climbed the stairs, stopping only when he noticed she wasn't shadowing him.

"I know the floor layout," he said by way of explanation. "Your brother didn't only hire my company to secure his company headquarters, but his home as well."

After seeing the extra measures of security outside, Anisa could see Ara had used Nasser's expertise well. Did she think it was necessary still? No, but as they headed up to the second floor, Anisa listened aptly while Nasser gave her a tour of the home security features.

"Certain areas of the home, mostly all entrance points, have a footstep detector. It'll send an alert to the control room and flag a security team to any movement."

He pointed to the vents they passed in the hallway. "There is a fogger system embedded into the ventilation of the home. When triggered, it blasts cold fog laced with a nonlethal compound at the intruder."

"What if it isn't an intruder?"

"The system can only be initiated with a series of authorizations and has remote activation capability."

"Seems excessive," she said with a shake of her head. "Next you'll tell me there's a remote weapons system embedded in the house."

Nasser was suspiciously quiet at that.

"There's a weapons system in the house!" Anisa didn't mask her shock, her voice loud and echoing in the hall.

"Behind the walls and embedded in the entrance hall ceiling and your brother's study, but again, access and activation would be near impossible without authorizations from both my company and Ara. You're safe from any perceived danger."

Safe?

She would feel far safer without knowing that the house was equipped to kill her.

Nasser paused and turned to her, his face a mask of severity. "No harm will come to you, not from the house or from anywhere else."

It was like a switch flipped, and her fear had been the trigger for the intensity in him that she hadn't yet grown used to. Her heart pitter-pattered, her stomach swooped, and her body warmed quickly and pleasantly. At the mercy of her physical reactions to Nasser, Anisa only breathed again when he resumed their tour.

"The walls, windows and doors are bulletproof and blast-proof. All the washrooms are equipped with biological washing systems."

"Why?" Anisa snapped her head away from admiring the beautiful tiling and luxurious bathroom amenities of one of the many bathrooms in one of the many bedrooms on that floor alone.

"Biochemical threats are still threats. Better prepared and vigilant than caught unaware and vulnerable."

She thought that nothing could top the extra feature in the bathrooms, at least not until Nasser said, "There's also a panic room on each floor."

"Of course there is," she muttered.

Right as Anisa began to think the surprises along the tour wouldn't cease, he walked her to the end of the long hall and opened the double doors at the end. Inside, the room was spacious and decorated in dark, muted tones. The flooring was a polished obsidian tile, the chairs a deep brown leather. A white area rug lay under a coffee table. On one side there was a sideboard, and on the other, a massive bookshelf that took up nearly the entire wall. But it was the far end of the room that caught her attention most. A grand executive desk of ebony wood, stainless steel, exquisite glass detailing, and touches of white leather panels and inserts.

She didn't need Nasser to confirm that this room belonged to Ara. Anisa could close her eyes and feel his presence permeating every surface of every piece of furniture, each crook and cranny, and even the walls.

"Your brother's study and office." Nasser strode over to the wide, floor-to-ceiling bookshelf, stepping off to the side. He brought Anisa's focus to a panel. "A thumb sensor—" he pressed his thumb to the digital reader "—and a passcode—" he punched in a series of digits "—protect this part of the full home security system."

The bookshelf she'd believed had been built into the wall suddenly parted down the middle, rolling in each direction before the shelves revealed a steel door with another security panel. Nasser went through the motions and revealed what lay beyond the impenetrable-looking door.

Anisa gaped at the high-tech monitors and paneling inside. "This main control unit is the gateway to every security feature in the home. Aside from your brother, my company personnel are the only ones with access to this area, in person and remotely."

She saw that he was waiting for her to come in closer, but Anisa backed away, suddenly overwhelmed. The shock of everything that had happened in the day was catching up to her. All of this, learning of Ara's hospitalization, returning home, discovering that her brother had spiraled into a paranoia—because how else could she explain the over-the-top security measures that seemed as much a threat to his person?—was too much to take in at once.

So she left.

Ran out of Ara's office and headed for the end of the hall, where, grasping the stairway railing, she peered down at the entrance hall and tried to slow her reeling mind.

What had her brother so fearful that he created a fortress out of their parents' home? In his quest to protect whatever it was Ara felt needed protection, he'd destroyed the memories and sentimental value this place held for her. When she looked around, she didn't see the faces of her *hooyo* and *aabo* anywhere.

Did he get rid of their belongings too?

With a clawing desperation, Anisa had to know. "My parents' room, where is it?"

She expected Nasser to tell her that no such room existed, but he turned on his heel and had her follow him to one of the closed rooms. He tried the handle with no success. After leaving her briefly to fetch a key, he returned and unlocked the room. Anisa's throat bobbed from her nerves, her socked feet dragging over the threshold, and her body trembling at the thought of what she would see.

Nasser flicked the light on. Besides a trace mustiness coming from the room, it looked exactly as she recalled it should.

The queen-sized bed with the old, scarred headboard, a mirror dresser still holding her mom's perfumes and jewelry boxes, the patterned Turkish rug that took up most of the floor, and so many other touches that swept her back to a time when her parents frequented this space.

"It looks the same," she sighed.

"He doesn't speak of this room often," Nasser said from behind her, his deep voice calm and even-toned, "but from what I've learned, he asked for it to be set up this way after the remodeling was completed and the interior decoration was happening."

Her relief at that was cut off shortly by fatigue.

Reading her mind, he gestured for her to follow him again. "Your room is this way."

Anisa stopped short at the threshold. It appeared that Ara hadn't only left their parents' personal belongings and furniture intact, but he'd enshrined her bedroom too. She walked in tentatively, taking in the familiar sights of her fuzzy baby blanket, her stuffed animals, the journals stacked on her small reading desk, and the DVDs and VHS tapes from her childhood neatly tucked in a media shelf beside the desk. On her bedside table was the heart-shaped trinket box her mother had bought for her ninth birthday.

My last birthday with them.

Anisa walked over to it, knowing that when she opened it, nothing would be inside. She hadn't had the heart to use it after her parents died. She'd tried to throw it away in an angry, grief-stricken state, but it had reappeared the very next day, rescued from being lost forever by Ara. He hadn't even scolded her about it.

She set the box down unopened, turning to Nasser and seeing that he had already placed her suitcase inside the room. Then he stood in the doorframe, watching her, as faithful and diligent in his duty to guard her as always.

Anisa appreciated that he'd been so understanding of her all through this journey. And now she knew that if she were to spill her guts to him, he wouldn't push her away. He'd seen her cry, shown her compassion and sympathy, and though he guarded his own secrets well, Anisa now felt that had more to do with personal issues he had to work through than any deficiency on her part.

But as much as she believed that speaking about her overwhelming emotions would make her feel better, she couldn't bring herself to do it. There was still so much for her to sort through on her own before she unloaded it on someone else.

"Do you need anything?"

His question pained her, mostly because she'd asked him to come along with her, and though Anisa didn't regret it, right in that moment she could have used time to herself. Nasser was trying to be helpful in his own way, but she hadn't signed up for him to hover over her.

"I just… I need to be alone."

Nasser didn't blink, nodding and making a move to leave her. Before he did, he reminded her, "I'll be downstairs if you need me."

Of that she had no doubt. But right then, and more than Ara, their parents, and Nasser, she just needed herself.

"Let me know if his condition changes in the slightest." Nasser ended the call with the hospital director personally handling Ara's care.

Feeling a crick in his neck, he stood for a stretch. He'd been seated behind Ara's desk, his laptop, tablet and phone all having been put through the wringer for the past twenty-four hours. Since having brought Anisa to her brother's home, and hearing that she hadn't wanted his company, Nasser had sealed himself in the office study and pored over his numerous work tasks. On top of all that, he'd answered several updates on Ara's welfare. He'd hoped to have better news for Anisa by now, but it was looking like time would be working against them.

For now, all he could do was to see that she stayed put in her childhood home.

And what of her comfort? a little voice chimed at him.

Nasser tensed at the memory of Anisa sending him away. She'd asked to be left alone, and he gave her the space she requested, barricading himself in the office to keep his mind off what felt like her rejection. He had only stepped out for mealtimes, always dropping in on Anisa to ensure that she joined him. Although he knew he could just as easily show her to the kitchen, or have Ara's personal chef whip up something for her and fetch a household staff member to deliver it to her room, it gave him additional peace of mind to have Anisa where he could see her.

*And maybe to touch her again...*that sneaky little voice taunted him.

Nasser shut it down before he cleared the office and headed out to pick Anisa up for breakfast.

She opened her bedroom door on the third sharp rap of his knuckles when he'd been one knock away from barging in.

"Join me for breakfast." He never framed it as a question, knowing that there could be a possibility for her to refuse him.

Stepping out wordlessly, and giving him a whiff of her sweet, floral perfume while she was at it, Anisa led him down to the cozy corner of the kitchen where a breakfast table with two seats and a tufted creamy white banquette sat beneath two small casement windows. The bright, airy light shone off the kitchen's warm neutral tones and added an enticing glow to her brown skin. She wore her lightweight, pale blue hijab in a more traditional style that circled her face.

But it was the thin, gold-wired, hexagonal-shaped glasses amplifying her shining dark eyes that had his heart kicking faster.

"You're wearing glasses," he commented lamely, too swept up in this change and in her general beauty to articulate himself any better. Nasser supposed it also wasn't a help that he hadn't slept last night. Worry that Anisa might need him, combined with a rattling longing to be by her side that had nothing to do with his guard duty, kept him up. The result was that his eyes itched and burned for sleep, and his body and mind were pushing the bounds of exhaustion. His answer to that was to pour himself a large mug full of black coffee, the dark, robust taste as rich and refreshing the first sip as it was when he refilled his mug for a second cup.

"I usually wear contacts, but they were hurting my eyes this morning." She shrugged. "Hence the glasses."

He didn't know what else to say, and she was lifting up the lids from the platters of their breakfast spread.

Nasser was displeased to see that her plate wasn't as full as he'd hoped it would be, but Anisa was eating what was in front of her, so he couldn't complain. He still worried when she sat back, apparently done eating her meal, and sipped gingerly at her coffee.

He hadn't seen her since dinner last night, and he was curious what kept her preoccupied in her room. As long as she wasn't crying in there…

"Any plans today?"

She gave another nonchalant shrug, her face eerily blank for her. "Nothing. Maybe I'll get some writing done."

"You're working?"

"No, I haven't picked up another gig yet. I just have time and figure I might as well work on my screenplay." She placed her mug down then, the first real emotion breaking through as she inquired softly, "Have you heard from Ara?"

"I spoke with the hospital's chief director. So far, all his preliminary tests have offered optimistic results. The director assures me that she'll continue to personally see to his care on top of your brother receiving round-the-clock attention from staff."

"But he hasn't woken up," deadpanned Anisa.

When he didn't respond, she excused herself and scooted out from the banquette seating.

Nasser gave her a few seconds' head start only because he was busy grinding his molars and berating himself on his poor handling of the situation. Then he scraped his chair back from the breakfast table and chased after her.

Anisa was halfway up the staircase when he called her back.

"Ara's still in a medical coma, but the director

reports that his prognosis is good." Not taking his eyes off her, he rooted his feet at the base of the stairs and fastened his hand on the railing to ease the urge to close the short distance to her. "He's going to be all right."

"You don't know that."

"No, you're right, nothing in health can be fully assured. And yet the tests all point towards an eventual recovery."

Anisa's soft sigh floated down to him. "I know you're trying to be helpful, and I do appreciate it, but I'll rest easier when he's woken from the coma." Then, without waiting for his response, she climbed the stairs and flitted off in the direction of her bedroom.

Nasser could have followed, though it'd be in vain. It was obvious she not only wished to be alone, but that his attempts at comfort weren't wanted either.

After breakfast, he went back to her brother's office and worked from there until noon, when a need for nourishment lured him outside the double doors of the study. He passed her room, slowed and faced her door. Funny how that slab of glossy, dark cherrywood had become an impenetrable fortress of its own.

Nasser forced himself to move on.

She wants to be all alone.

And that was fine by him.

He had to look at the bright side: as long as she

stayed indoors, he didn't have to work twice as hard as he'd done in Madagascar to protect her. This way, half his work was being done by the security features his company integrated into the house.

Yet despite his resolve to leave her be, Nasser returned from a quick, lonely lunch only to hover in front of her door again.

There he had a debate with himself on whether he should knock and try to rouse her from her room, or walk on and continue pretending he wasn't immensely perturbed by her decision to lock herself up.

What if she's crying again?

And he wouldn't know, because he was standing outside instead of being with her. Nasser clenched his fists, wishing he could see through the door, if only to ensure she wasn't wrapped up in abject misery. He flexed his hands and tensed his muscles, battling these opposing sides of him to ignore her wishes and act, or do as she requested and remain still.

Finally, and with his feet feeling as though they were encased in cement shoes, he walked away from her bedroom door. Nasser had taken two heavy steps when a lock unlatching sounded from behind him. He spun back just as Anisa stepped out, her head rising and her eyes finding him.

For several heartbeats, neither of them said a word.

Nasser could've contented himself by merely

gazing at her and confirming that—at least on the outside—she looked all right. More than all right, it appeared as though she were headed outdoors, a sun hat in her hand, sunglasses perched on her head, and a large, floppy purse strapped over her shoulder.

"Where are you going?" He kept his face smooth of the nervousness now pinging through him.

It was true that he hadn't liked it when she confined herself in her room, but Nasser hadn't wanted her to go out, where protecting her would be that much more challenging. Worse, the thought that she might not want him to go with her struck him.

How will I keep her safe then?

Normally, he'd have pushed past her protests as he had in Madagascar. The biggest difference between then and now was that they weren't the same people they'd been when they first met. At least not to each other. Now he was more familiar with her. It felt downright rotten of him to ignore her wishes and force his protection on her.

Even if it's for her own good?

Nasser's jaw hardened, knowing that despite what was good for her, he would still probably cave to her desires.

He knew that if she asked to be alone again this time, he would do his best to allow it, maybe order security personnel to trail her from afar in his stead. But Nasser delivered a quiet prayer that it wouldn't come to that.

"The beach," Anisa said after a short silence.

He was fully expecting her to then tell him that she'd like to be by herself.

"Did you want to come with me?" she asked.

He couldn't have heard her invitation correctly, yet when she stood there staring at him expectantly, he realized with a jolt that, *yes*, not only had she invited him on her day excursion, but Anisa was waiting on his answer.

Not that she has to ask…

"Oui." And Nasser didn't think he relished saying a word more.

CHAPTER TEN

THERE WAS SOMETHING about being in the sunlight with her feet squishing in the wet sand and the ocean lapping her wriggling toes that put a smile on her face.

"That feels so good," Anisa moaned as she lifted her face to the sun and the heat penetrated her bones and thawed some of the chill that had been clinging to her over the past few days. She stretched her arms up over her head and arched back, the tension unwinding from her muscles as slowly and gently as the tide rushing up over the sand before scurrying back off the shore. "I could stand here all day."

"It is peaceful here," Nasser said.

At the sound of his voice, Anisa lowered her arms and peered up at him from behind her sunglasses. He wouldn't be able to see her eyes fully, and somehow that made it easier to face him and hide from her guilty conscience. She'd been rudely brushing off his kind gestures since they arrived at her home.

Is it really still my *home, though?*

Anisa couldn't completely rid herself of the idea that, despite Ara having preserved her parents' belongings and hers as well, she no longer belonged here with him. The fear that she didn't fit in in the one place where she should have—that's what kept her locked away in her room. She'd barely slept because of it too. It was only here, on this quiet sprawl of shore, that she'd finally felt her overactive thoughts drop from a shout to the softest of whispers.

She wasn't in a hurry to give up the rare peace so quickly.

Yet…she had to.

Though she didn't owe Nasser anything, when Anisa had asked him for some space, he had given it to her. Sure, he would pull her out of her room for meals. But that only showed he cared enough to not let her starve. And because he'd been hired to watch over her, it couldn't have been easy for him to stand back. She was grateful to him for overriding his natural protective instinct and respecting her request to be left alone.

It was the reason she'd invited Nasser to the beach with her.

I had time to myself.

Now she was ready to talk.

"Nasser," she began to say, just as he said, "Anisa."

They stopped and stared at each other.

Anisa brushed off her surprise and laughed lightly. "We must have been thinking the same thing."

"I suppose we were," he concurred with a small smile. "You can speak first."

Anisa nodded, her good humor stifled now that the spotlight was on her. Her hands only slightly trembling, she pulled the sunglasses off her face, feeling like she needed to look him in the eye for what she had to say—even if losing the shades left her more vulnerable than ever.

"I'm sorry."

He blinked slowly at her apology, his non-reaction exacerbating her nerves.

"I knew coming home would be hard in some ways. I just didn't anticipate just how difficult it would be." Anisa knew nothing she could've done would have prepared her for her homecoming. True, it might have been easier had her return not been prompted by Ara's injury, but the same doubts and concerns would have followed her around.

"You have to understand Ara hasn't spoken to me in years, yet he still kept my bedroom the same for me. What am I supposed to think?"

Nasser remained silent up until that point, but now he said, "You don't need to apologize for the way you feel, Anisa. Although I can't speak for your brother or explain his logic, perhaps it's his way of showing he cares."

"If he truly cared, he would have picked up his phone and sent a text or called, or heck, done *both*," she argued, scoffing. It was already painful to think about Ara snubbing her these past four years, but to have Nasser defend him added salt to the wound.

"Maybe he was afraid."

She raised her brows. "Of?"

"You might not have answered his calls or messages."

Anisa pondered that, and her anger flowed away as quickly as it filled her up. Staring down at her feet, her curling toes squelching in the sand, she recalled the fury she'd first felt when she had moved away and Ara had cut off communication with her in retaliation. If he had tried talking to her while she'd been that angry, then Anisa knew she wouldn't have been very kind to him. Of course her irritation had cooled as the years passed, and she began to miss Ara more than loathe his choice to push her away.

But he doesn't know that.

How could he when they hadn't spoken for all this time?

"Okay, I see what you mean," she said, looking up from her feet and smiling at him. Nasser made a solid argument, and though she didn't know if he intended to soften her heart toward Ara, he succeeded. "I only hope my brother's paying you well enough," she teased.

Nasser's husky laughter was worth it.

Like his smiles, his mirth seemed a rare treasure to cherish. And Anisa did just that, quietly.

"Did you want to go for a walk?" he asked, tipping his head toward the lonely stretch of beach. It was quiet this time of day when the sun was hottest and most people were at home having *asariya*—their afternoon tea.

Anisa had chosen that hour for a specific reason.

Grinning, she sifted through the open top of her oversized tote bag and pulled out what she was searching for: a spool of fishing line already equipped with a hook. Lowering her tote bag by her sandals and wading into the ocean with the fishing line in hand, she glanced back at Nasser and almost laughed at the frown on his face. "How about we fish for our lunch instead?" she asked him.

For the next half hour, Anisa reeled in a couple fish and collected them in a small bucket she had pulled out of her tote. Standing still at the edge of the water, Nasser appeared content to keep an eye on her from the shore. He didn't make a move to join her or even ask her questions.

Tiring of the silence, she stopped beside him and held out the fishing line.

"Why do I feel like I'm the only one working for our meal?" she joked. "Come on, let's see you try. Unless you're scared to get wet." Anisa eyed his perfect-looking suit and polished shoes.

He looked so good, Anisa understood why he wasn't jumping into the cold grip of the ocean. When he didn't accept the line from her, she shrugged off her disappointment and waded back into the water.

She was tugging at the line, slowly reeling it in, when Nasser stepped up beside her, his hand outstretched.

Anisa gawked at him, her eyes trailing down to where he'd rolled the cuff of his pants up to the middle of his calves. It did little good—the ocean still drenched him. Shaking off her stupor, she passed him the fishing line and focused on showing him where his hands should be. She wasn't going to be distracted by the feel of his fingers as she pried them just loose enough for the line to slip through when he reeled in his catch. Or his hard bicep as she showed him how to hold his arm up and pull the reel in with sharp tugs. And she certainly wasn't going to lean into the fluttery heat when his body bumped hers, his eyes flicking down to her face and flashing with awareness at their dangerously close proximity.

Blushing, Anisa shied back from him and stammered, "Y-you're holding it right. Now just let the fish come to you."

She was still caught up in her attraction to him, but not as strongly by the time Nasser snagged his first fish. Anisa cheered for him, guiding him back to the beach and showing him how to pull the fish off the hook before adding his catch to hers.

They made two more trips with only one other catch before Anisa called it a day. Sitting down on the beach blanket she spread out for them, she checked on the fish in the bucket and beamed proudly at him. "We caught way more than I thought we would."

Nasser smiled back. "I had a good instructor."

"I was pretty good, wasn't I?"

He chuckled at her boast, and then surprised her when he asked, "Did your brother teach you to fish?"

"No, Ara and I both learned to fish from our parents." Anisa wiped wet sand off fish scales, reminiscing about the last time she'd gone fishing with her whole family, so many years ago now. "There's a nine-year age gap between Ara and me, so he learned to fish first. Most of the time I was too young to join him and my father in the ocean, so I would wait on the shore with my mom. Then I'd help her clean the fish before we hauled our catch of the day home."

She smiled to herself, the memories now coming back to her. "When we weren't fishing, I used to walk this beach with my mother and father. Ara and I were always running after each other, making up games, playing in the sand or ocean, sometimes both.

"I thought it would be hard coming back here, too, but it isn't," she confessed, lowering the fish she'd been holding, her bottom lip trembling as she looked out at the ocean. "I thought I'd be scared of the ocean after what it took from me, but I'm not."

"Is this where it happened?"

Anisa sucked in her lips and managed to nod once, slow. After she admitted to the hardest part, the rest of the events leading up to that awful day came tumbling from her mouth.

"Ara was away on a school field trip, and I couldn't wait for him to get home to play with me, so I begged my parents to take us boating.

"Even though they were both busy, they stopped what they were doing and took us out on the small fishing boat my dad owned."

Anisa felt a smile, small and fragile, lift her lips. "I loved touching the ocean." She could feel her dad's arms around her middle as he helped her reach for the waves, and she could see her mother's beautiful smile and hear her sparkling laughter as Anisa and her dad flicked water at her. "But even more than that, I loved spending time with them.

"We were so busy laughing, it seemed that my parents missed the boat careening straight toward us. My dad tried to wave for their attention, but it happened so fast. They clipped us, and our boat upended." Anisa touched a hand to her middle, swearing that she felt the phantom press of her mother's arm tightly winding around her as they went under together. She never saw her dad again, but she had clung to her mom for as long as she could.

"I was found on the beach alone. When I couldn't find my mom or dad, I remember running out into the ocean, crying for them. The people who found me stopped me from going in any deeper.

"Later, when Ara finally arrived at the hospital, I learned my mom had washed up only a little further down the beach. She was gone, but the rescue team thought that she'd saved me." Anisa's eyes watered, and no matter how fast she blinked, she felt the tears burgeoning. "My dad washed up later. I can't stop thinking that he died alone, and that she died to rescue me."

Anisa cried quietly, her cheeks growing wetter by the second. And when it became too much, she turned away, her hands too dirty to cover her face, but her pain too ready for her to look into Nasser's eyes anymore.

That was why she was unprepared when his hand covered hers on the beach mat, his fingers squeezing and coaxing warmth into her. Shocked and blinking back tears, she saw that he had moved closer to comfort her. Without thinking, she leaned into him, pressed her face into his chest and cried on him. To his credit, Nasser's hands settled over her shoulders. He held her gently, letting her work out the pain deep inside that she'd unburied. He hugged her back, and Anisa couldn't put into words how good it felt in her moment of grieving.

It felt like ages had passed when she finally stirred against his hard chest and peered up, her eyes sore and her vision still misty, but her heart no longer hurting as badly. She must have looked a mess, but she didn't feel it, not with the way Nasser was gazing at her. His eyes lowered to her mouth. She licked her lips instinctively, dragging her tongue across her lower lip, and watching his eyebrows furrow and his own mouth harden into a scowl.

They were pressed scandalously close, chancing the possibility of someone seeing them.

She was going to point out that they needed to separate, but her hands clung to the front of his shirt, his chest warm and solid under her palms, and her body buzzing with the knowledge that he wanted this too. Anisa could see it in the way he stared at her like he was starved and she was the only one who could feed the hunger.

If she had any doubt that he desired her, it was eliminated when he inched his face lower and closer to hers.

Anisa's breath hitched in sweetest expectation.

The last time they had a moment like this, Nasser had pulled away from her and left her with a heavy disappointment that still pressed down on her. What made it doubly worse was that he'd only stopped to answer the call relaying the news of her brother's injury and hospitalization.

After that experience, she felt shakier that it might happen all over again.

So she couldn't be blamed when her fingers dug into his shirtfront to keep him from running off on her again. Anisa then counted the seconds, her eyelids fluttering lower and her face angling up to his. She didn't have to wait long to finally feel him the way she'd yearned to since Madagascar.

Nasser's mouth pressed down on hers, tentatively at first, almost as though he wouldn't risk harming her, but that changed quickly.

Making a noise that was a cross between a growl and a groan, Nasser dropped his hands down her arching back and hauled her against him. Anisa's gasp was swallowed up in their passionate kiss. Shutting off her mind, she closed her eyes and gave back as good as he was giving her. She had kissed only one person before, and that had been years ago when she'd been a young teenager innocently exploring her feelings. Nothing had come of it, and that kiss would never compare to the maturity and expertise behind Nasser's mastery of her mouth.

Within moments he had her melting into a goopy puddle in his arms.

"Anisa," he rasped against her, his warm

breath heating her jawline as he scored her with his hot lips.

Needing him higher up, she framed his face with her hands, the bristly shadow of a beard on his jaw tickling her palms and heightening her pleasure. She lifted him to her and locked lips with him again. The way this kiss curled her toes had Anisa realizing how much more this meant to her than the simple satisfaction of a desire.

I like him.

She liked Nasser a lot, and Anisa knew she'd have to do something about it later, but right then all she wanted and needed was for him to hold her tighter and kiss her breathless.

Kissing Anisa wasn't a mistake in and of itself...

No, I don't think I'll ever regret it.

But now Nasser wasn't sure what to do about the feelings their intimate moment unlocked.

Because she was everywhere for him after their passionate display on the beach. Under his skin, in each and every tug of his heart, and in the heat coiling below his belt. No matter how many times he told himself it shouldn't happen again if he valued what was best for her, he would look down to where her head rested on his shoulder, and he'd forget everything except the achingly sweet memory of his mouth slotted perfectly over hers.

It hadn't surprised him that they fit so well together. In a way, they'd been dancing around this attraction of theirs for some time.

That doesn't mean we had to act on it.

He must have sighed. He couldn't think of another reason why Anisa would lift her head off his shoulder and look up at him, her eyes roaming over his face, curiosity creasing her brow.

"Are you having second thoughts?" she asked, discerning where his mind had gone.

"Are you?"

"I don't really know what to say."

Nasser tensed at the indecisiveness threading her words, and he only relaxed when Anisa continued, "But I do know that I can't regret what happened."

Relieved, he nodded in agreement. "Then we share that sentiment."

"I'm glad…" Anisa trailed off, picking up after a quick sigh. "It's hard talking about my parents. Thinking of their deaths is painful. Sometimes I wonder why I didn't die with them. Why them and not me?" She drew her legs up closer to her body, her arms wrapped over her knees and her gaze pointed at the ocean spread out before them.

Why Nuruddin and not him?

How often had he wondered that?

Knowing the guilt she was living through quite intimately, he needn't have imagined what she was thinking or feeling, because he experienced it every time he thought of his brother. No amount of logic had ever been able to spare him the grief and burden of being the one left behind.

The one who was saved.

Maybe that was why, without any comforting words at the ready, he pried his pinched lips apart and cracked open the steel doors on his well-guarded past.

"When my brother, Nuruddin, passed away, I often questioned why it hadn't been me in his place. He was better to our parents, good at his studies, a *hafiz*, and he had a dream of using his good heart and smart brain to help the world.

"He was everything I wasn't at the time. And it never made sense to me why he died and why I was spared."

"Spared?" Anisa's brows pinched closer together, and the ocean lost her attention as she focused on him. "What do you mean?"

Nasser unclenched his jaws and said, "He died at a protest rally against the corruption within the government."

He'd never be able to scrub that day clean from his mind, and now he was reliving it as he played the events back for Anisa.

"Along with a group of his friends, they marched in Hargeisa and faced off against a hostile military force in the city for the protests. I had gone with him, not thinking that I'd leave without him."

Anisa's face crumpled at that part, and he paused,

gathering his own emotions in the face of her sadness for him.

In a thicker voice, he said, "The military officials weren't supposed to do anything more than supervise, but less than an hour into the peaceful demonstrations, they started brutalizing protestors. A fight broke out, and it was us versus them. Everyone was either charging headfirst into the fray or running in the opposite direction.

"When the situation turned for the worse, Nuruddin grabbed my hand and was pulling me away, but I—"

He had to break off, a bilious swell of emotion sticking fast in his throat. Waiting while it worked itself down gradually, Nasser responded to Anisa's searching fingers touching his fisted hand over the small space between them on her beach mat. She caressed his knuckles, her eyes on his face, concern for his emotional welfare etching frown lines around her mouth and between her fine dark eyebrows. When he didn't move away from her, she placed her hand on his, blanketing his fist and calming the prickly feelings needling his insides.

With that touch, she gave him the strength to say what troubled him most. "I feel responsible for his death."

Nasser could see it as though he were living through it all over again. Nuruddin's hand in his own, his brother's panicked features filling his vision...

"We have to go, Nasser!"

His brother pulled sharply on his hand, dragging him away from the clash of protestors against the armored body shields of the military officers.

Fire erupted from a car nearby, glass crunched beneath his feet, and some of the boards scrawled with protest slogans nearly tripped him.

He would have fallen if Nuruddin hadn't helped right him quickly.

"Why can't we stay?" Nasser cried. "They aren't really going to hurt us, are they?"

"Even if they don't, we can't be here anymore. It's not safe," his brother shouted over the noise.

In the present, Nasser continued his tale, unable to stop the floodgates he'd opened. "He tried to get us away, but I didn't want to leave. Not yet."

"Look, Nuruddin! They're hurting those people."

Nasser pointed out two men holding boards in front of their bodies protectively as the military advanced with batons, battering anyone who stood in their path. One of the men toppled backwards, and as soon as he was on the ground, the board was ripped out of his hand. He was battered by half a dozen military officers' solid batons.

They beat him relentlessly, his cries echoing down the streets.

Nasser shuddered in real time, his body growing cold and hot simultaneously as the nightmarish memory haunted him once more.

"My brother," he continued hoarsely, "he wanted to protect me, but I couldn't leave well enough alone. He followed me into the fray, and we fought off the officers with boards we'd picked up from the ground. We weren't alone. Before we knew it, we were at the epicenter of a battle between protestors and so-called officers of the peace." He spat the word, his hatred revitalized for the cruel-faced men brandishing their batons, big shields, and bigger guns. If he could round every one of them up today and wreak his vengeance on them, he would. Because what happened after changed his life irrevocably…

"Nasser!" Nuruddin cried out his name as Nasser was ripped away from his side by some of the military officials. "Nasser!" he yelled one last time.

Then there was a series of ear-shattering bangs followed by an eerie silence that could've stopped Nasser's heart.

In an out-of-body moment, and still gripped tightly by the officers who had grabbed hold of him and hauled them over onto their side, Nasser watched his brother slacken and collapse to the ground.

"They shot him. I tried to save him. Tried, but I knew." He swallowed hard, the memory of cradling his brother's lifeless body after he'd managed to wrench free of his captors paining him physically. "I knew he was gone.

"After Nuruddin died, crowd control was swift. The protestors either were subdued or ran away." Those who hadn't managed to escape were caught and carted off to jail, and he was one of the unlucky dozen or so. "Nuruddin was the only one who'd died. Many more were injured.

"And it wouldn't have happened if I had listened to him. He would still be here."

With me.

And with their parents, who still grieved their eldest son, a son Nasser couldn't ever replace.

He was finished, and he sat in silence after that, drained emotionally and feeling hollow. He didn't know if he liked the emptiness left behind, but Nasser supposed it was better than having memories choke him up any longer. And if he hadn't said anything, Anisa wouldn't have had a reason to comfort him with her touch. He stared at their point of contact, right now the only thing tethering him in reality. He'd worried that if he trudged through his unpleasant memories, he would get mired down by them. But he hadn't.

Through it all, Anisa hadn't said anything. Now he was done, she said, "I'm sorry for your brother. Sorry for you, too. You must have been young, because I don't remember a violent protest happening in Hargeisa."

"I was fifteen." Seeing by the way her brows puckered and her lips pooched adorably that she was doing the math of their ages, he helped her out. "You would've been nine, I believe."

"The same age my parents died… It wasn't a good year for either of us then."

He couldn't disagree.

The sad look on Anisa's face matched the sorrow darkening his mind. He blamed himself for upsetting her after she'd already cried not too long ago. He then recalled the reason why he'd even opened up, remembering that he had tried to share in her sympathy and return the trust she'd offered him in speaking about her parents. It had hurt telling her of his brother's final moments, but Nasser couldn't deny that he wasn't as burdened anymore.

Oddly, he felt better now that she knew.

He didn't understand what that meant, only that his heart didn't feel as cold and unreachable when Anisa pressed their palms together and laced her fingers through his. In fact, for the first time since losing Nuruddin, talking about his brother didn't inflict him with the usual grief and guilt.

CHAPTER ELEVEN

NASSER DIDN'T THINK Anisa could surprise him after the unexpected fishing trip, but when they left the beach, she led him to a restaurant where they handed their fish to staff and had their catch of the day prepared for lunch.

It was a unique experience made all the sweeter by Anisa's smiles and laughter. Seeing her happier did his heart a world of good. She hadn't had much reason to be lighthearted these past few days, with her brother being hospitalized and then having to confront the ghosts she'd left behind in Berbera. Nasser knew it couldn't have been easy.

If it were, I would have done it myself.

Going home was a sore topic for him too. He loved his parents, and it wasn't their fault that he couldn't stand to be home for very long, not with the memories of Nuruddin haunting the rooms and corridors of their house.

That was why he was proud of Anisa. In facing her grief, she did something that he couldn't.

They had come a long way from her fighting

his protection. She might have only graced his life for a little more than a week, yet in that short time she'd made a big impact on him. The kind that he'd never be able to forget.

The kind he didn't *want* to forget.

After lunch, aiming to take her home, he slowed his truck when Anisa stopped pointing out the places she used to frequent regularly while growing up in that city. She simply stared out the car window. He followed the line of her vision to a small but seemingly popular supermarket, if the crowd in line out the door was anything to go by.

"Our parents would take Ara and me to this market all the time for ice cream bars after a long, hot day of fishing together."

He didn't have to ask, but he did. "Would you like ice cream?" He left out that they'd had a long, hot day of their own on the beach.

It got pretty hot near the end too, didn't it?

Unwilling to follow where that thought led him, Nasser instructed her to wait in the car for him. "I won't be long," he promised.

In the end, he baked outdoors under the sun and at the very end of the line into the supermarket for a solid ten minutes. When he was finally able to navigate the store, there was little choice of ice creams. He had to settle for what was left: two mint chocolate chip sandwich bars. Not his most favorite flavor, but he prayed Anisa was satisfied since she'd requested a chocolate ice cream.

Another line slowed him down at the checkout lane. Though he was antsy to get back to her, he kept a grip on his patience by anticipating the joy on Anisa's pretty face once he passed her the sweet treat.

He had just reached the cashier when a commotion outside drifted in. Peering out the front glass of the store, he saw a crowd gathering on the street.

Frowning, he left behind his change in his hurry to pay for the ice cream, his instincts telling him that he needed to be outside.

And his gut didn't fail him, because he immediately saw that Anisa and his truck were surrounded by strangers. Someone had thrown a large stone onto the hood of his vehicle.

Nasser halted, a mix of shock and adrenaline locking his muscles before his blood heated and he unfroze. The first thing he did once he was free was to run toward Anisa and assess the situation, clocking all the relevant details. The stone had cratered the windshield and part of the hood. But the damage wasn't the foremost item on his mind. Intercepting any more threats to her leaped to the top of his priority list. If he had to whisk her away to keep her safe, then so be it.

Glowering at the curious onlookers, he ushered Anisa into the truck and passed her the ice creams he'd managed not to crush in his angry fright. He hauled the stone off the truck and onto the sidewalk before he slipped into the driver's seat and got them out of there as fast as possible.

He drove out of the city and to the outskirts where her home was in record time. All during the drive, out of the corner of his eye, he noticed Anisa holding on tightly to the handlebar. She slowly let it go when he finally parked the truck behind the well-guarded enclosure of her family property.

Unbuckling his seat belt, he opened the car door and waited for her to do the same.

When she didn't move a muscle and stared unblinkingly out the cracked windshield, he faced her. "Let's go inside and decompress."

She followed him slowly into the house, shock seeming to have totally numbed her into silence.

Up to that point, he'd placed her safety before his curiosity, but now that he had her secured in her home, Nasser asked for details.

"What happened?"

She shook her head as if rousing from a reverie before whipping her head to him. "A young boy threw the stone and started shouting at me. He said that Ara sent his father to prison. When I said that couldn't be true, he told me that Ara had his father falsely accused of embezzling public funds from his office."

Nasser folded his arms, furious that he'd left her alone and exposed to danger but tabling his anger to ask, "How did he know Ara was your brother?"

"His mother was there, too. I…recognized her. She was one of my mother's friends, and she used to visit often back in the day." Anisa bit her lip, her anguish palpable in her voice when she asked, "What they said can't be true, right? Ara couldn't have sent an innocent man away."

"If he sent him away, he likely wasn't innocent."

Anisa's mouth dropped open. "Okay, but why would Ara even get involved?"

"Your brother's sense of justice is strong. That and he has the wealth and power to stand up to corruption. Of course that means he's made enemies."

"Enemies?" Anisa spoke the word slowly, like she was tasting the syllables in her mouth and then pruning her lips at the distaste.

"It might seem like exaggeration, but these enemies of his could pose a threat to you simply by association." As she surely had just witnessed herself. "In the meantime, we should remain indoors, out of sight—"

"You mean *I* should remain indoors and out of sight," she interjected.

Nasser quelled a sigh. He had thought they'd moved past this. Her distrust cut deeper now though.

Because I kissed her.

And because of it, he had a pain in his heart that was projected in his sharp tone. "If it means safeguarding your well-being, then yes. Indoors and out of sight."

"And if I refuse?"

"You'd be foolish," he snapped, already irritated at the incident in the city. Her unwillingness to protect herself was the last straw.

Anisa's shock at his comment wore off rapidly, her anger storming over her face. "Then let me be foolish. Why do you care?"

"Your brother hired me to do a job—"

"A job that ended when I decided to come home."

She was technically right, but also wrong. "The job was for me to protect you until you left for Canada, and since you have yet to do that…" He let the rest of his explanation stand, seeing no way for her to argue against the logic he'd placed before her.

"What's the point of protecting me if you're going to lock me up instead? You did a fine enough job in Madagascar. Why does it have to be different here?"

Her confidence in him was touching, but the truth was that he hadn't done a very good job at protecting her just now. And she must have sensed his self-doubt in his silence because she gentled her voice.

"I just don't understand why you're being so cautious. You saved me. Isn't that enough?"

Okay, so he saved her this time, only because he was able to intercept the danger to her.

But what about next time?

What if he couldn't get to her in time to rescue her? Then what? Nasser would've failed her. Failed himself.

Just like I failed Nuruddin.

Another person lost to his inability to protect those who mattered to him. Those he loved—

Love? Where had that come from? He didn't love Anisa. He *couldn't* love her.

He had no right to it, not if he couldn't protect her.

Anisa approached him, sealing the gap between them, and infiltrating his senses with the sweet sultriness of her perfume. He took in her full, glossy lips, small, pointed chin, upturned nose and round, dark eyes that reflected his uncertainty back at him. He wavered between taking her in his arms and walking away from the temptation—*no*, the promise that she presented him.

"Nasser, you can protect me. You have. There's nothing to worry about."

"Anisa, I…can't."

What happened on the beach had to stay on the beach. The only other place it could exist was in their memories. She thought she knew him simply because he shared the last moments of his brother with her, but she had no clue of the depth of anger, the hunger for revenge her brother promised him, or the real reason why fate had crossed and then tied their paths.

If she only knew...

She wouldn't be looking at him with that clueless softness of hers.

The anger he kept bottled really was no different than the young man who had come at his truck with a stone. The kind of rage that started young only built on itself, calcifying to a point of no return, and turning one's heart as hard as the stone that cracked his windshield and dented his truck's hood. He could have easily done that if he were facing the culprits who had killed his brother. Not the military officials who had been ordered to violently disrupt the protest, but the true puppeteers behind the cruel carnage that stole Nuruddin's life.

That's what I have to focus on.

With that firmly in mind, Nasser turned away from her. "Since we don't seem to be getting along or seeing eye to eye, I'll leave you." Then, having never taken off his shoes, he grabbed the handle, opened the front door, and walked out of the house before he decided walking away from Anisa was a mistake.

The coward.

The low-down, no-good coward.

Anisa quietly stewed for days after discovering

that Nasser had called it quits on her and passed her protection detail to one of his employees.

Like a hot potato, she observed sourly.

She might have accepted that he hadn't wanted to deal with her anymore *if* he'd had the common decency to tell her that much.

Instead, he'd relegated some other guy to do his job for him. The new guy, Daniel, was nice and seemed capable enough, and he'd told her that he had the pleasure of working closely with her brother. Anisa was admittedly intrigued by that, but it didn't let Nasser off the hook.

She was cross with him.

At first she'd wanted to hunt him down and shout his ears off, but then she realized that no one would allow her off the property on Nasser's explicit orders. Even if she could manage to sneak off, Anisa didn't have a clue where Nasser had gone. A quick, simple internet search mentioned that he had homes in several places all over the world. She wouldn't know where to begin to look.

Why am I chasing after him?

It was so apparent that he didn't care about her at all. Not in the way she imagined and hoped he would.

Lying in her bed, flat on her back, she touched her lips, the soft pads of her fingers sadly not a comparison to the immense pleasure his mouth had given her. Anisa sighed and dropped her hand away, resting it on her chest over her thumping heart. She sat up when her thoughts wouldn't let her relax. Moving over to her small writing desk, she picked up the empty notebook she'd found and begun writing in. It was a first draft of an idea that she had started kicking around in her head.

She hadn't attempted a screenplay in over a year now. Her work, paying off her student loans, and the rent on her apartment had become her priority. But now, with all the free time she had after Nasser basically ran off on her, Anisa had drifted back to the haven her creativity once offered her.

And it was looking like it would be a good distraction for her again. Sitting down, she picked up her pen.

She poured her emotions onto the page. Letting out the frustration, anguish, pining and every other tumultuous feeling she couldn't name while she created her world, characters, and plot in a frenzied daze.

By the time she lifted her head, it was nearly midnight. Her body ached, her brain shutting down for the day, the thoughts of Ara's well-being, Nasser's sudden abandonment, and what the future held for all of them no longer tormenting her. It was only then that Anisa pulled herself away from her desk and all the words she'd written and crawled into her bed with nothing on her mind but a wish for a good night's sleep.

She lived in isolation like that for three days

and nights after Nasser handed his protection duty over to his staff.

Anisa anticipated nothing would change on the fourth day.

And nothing had in the beginning, her day unfolding the same. But sometime in the late evening, she was distracted from her writing when noises in the hallway dragged her over to her closed bedroom door. Tiptoeing over as the unmistakable sound of heavy foot treads passed, she placed her ear to the door, stilled her heavy breathing and listened.

The footfalls receded down the corridor in the direction of her brother's study. This was followed by the faint click of a door latch being unlocked.

Anisa pulled back, staring hard at the door.

Who had the keys to her brother's study besides Nasser? And if that was him, why was he skulking around the house so late like a thief in the night?

Duh. He's trying to avoid me.

Anisa seethed at that.

She'd done nothing to him to deserve this treatment. And who kissed someone and just up and pretended like nothing happened?

Heartless jerk.

Bristling, Anisa flung open her bedroom door, determined to corner him and tell him exactly how awful he was making her feel.

The house was incredibly still—the kind of

stillness that carried its own kind of noise. She could hear her heartbeats clearer, as well as her breathing, and the creak of the hardwood floorboards beneath the carpet runner spanning the long corridor.

What if isn't Nasser but an intruder?

She hadn't really considered that, and it gave her pause. But she realized it would be a next to impossible feat for any intruder, what with all the guards, and all the cameras stationed outside and inside the home and equipped with fancy heat vision, not to mention the sensor wires that Nasser had told her were running along the property so no one could walk in without being detected.

Feeling that the likelihood of it being a burglar or some other nefarious character was slim, Anisa snapped her shoulders back and steeled her spine as she closed in on the double doors to her brother's study. Her heart rate picked up when she heard footfalls inside, like someone was in there pacing. A shadow slid past the crack of light streaming from under the doors. She grasped the door handle. Before she could talk herself out of barging in, she flung open the door.

It was just as Anisa expected, her eyes finding and landing on Nasser the instant she stepped into the room. She recognized him even with the darker stubble masking his jaw. Triumph drummed in her chest when he appeared taken aback by the sight of her, his eyes doubling in size.

She opened her mouth, ready to count all the ways he'd hurt her with his sudden departure, but ended up swallowing her words as she heard her name.

"Anisa?"

That voice—she would've recognized it blindfolded despite not hearing it for four years now.

Ara.

Anisa hadn't looked the whole room over when she marched in. Now that she did, she could easily see her brother sitting behind his big, opulent desk, bathed in the golden glow of his desk lamp. "You're awake," he said, proving that he was there. In the flesh. Alive and whole and looking like himself despite sitting in a wheelchair, a bandage wound around his head and neck and another one plastered to his left cheek.

The bandage covering his face didn't hinder him from smiling.

It was a slight upward tilt of his lips, but Anisa would take it. Whenever she dreamed of this encounter, it was always with the worry that he would look at her in the same cold way he'd done when she had chosen to move out of their family home.

He's here. He's really here, and he's smiling at me.

Anisa couldn't express the jolt of emotions that seized her all at once. Her overflowing joy seemed to have no end.

"Ara." Her voice broke as she said his name. Anisa swiped at her cheeks and felt the wetness on them. She took a jerky step forward, and then another one.

Looking like he intended to meet her halfway, Ara rolled toward her, grunting as he did, not able to entirely mask the pain tightening his hard-planed face. He stopped in front of her, locked the wheels and slowly pulled himself to a stand. Anisa fought the urge to help him. Not knowing if her touch would awaken a grudge in him, she held herself back. Because now that her fear for his life was extinguished, she feared losing him to his anger at her just as she had all this time they hadn't communicated.

So she left Ara to stand on his own two feet and in his own good time.

"You shouldn't overexert yourself," Nasser cautioned him. "The doctor said—"

Nasser's warning was cut short by Ara's scoff.

"I heard what the doctor said." Panting, he pulled his hands off the armrests of the wheelchair and stood with the teeniest of wobbles. He gave her a nod and another small smile, but he spoke to Nasser when he said, "I think just this once, the doctor will forgive me if I want to hug my sister without having her crouch to my level."

Anisa's bottom lip trembled as Ara opened his arms to her. In that instant, she knew that their relationship was on its way to healing and maybe even improving from what it was.

He hugged her tightly and whispered at her ear, "I missed you, baby sis."

Face buried in his shoulder, Anisa cried at that, and one loud sob that couldn't be completely muffled escaped. She bawled so hard she shook in his arms. When she finally settled down enough to draw back, her face wet from her teary display, Anisa could see that Ara hadn't remained unaffected either.

His eyes shone with unshed tears as he gave her another crooked smile.

"I missed you too," Anisa said.

More than you'll ever know...

Giving her another nod, his face lined with fatigue, he gazed at her with understanding. They might have stood like that, his arms still around her, if Ara hadn't suddenly gone heavy in her arms. Anisa cried out, nearly toppling down to the floor with Ara's body weight crushing her. Nasser came to her rescue.

Together, they eased Ara back down into his wheelchair.

Over her brother's head, she caught Nasser's eyes briefly, his nostrils flaring at her as he seemed to drink her in. And she hated that with one look he obliterated her upset with him and set her body alight with longing. Giving her head a shake, Anisa looked away. The only thing that would sting more than Nasser's abandonment was Ara discovering that there was more going on between her and Nasser than a simple protector-protectee relationship.

Now safely seated, Ara grunted, reminding her that he wasn't fully healed. That despite having made it home to her, her brother had a long journey to full recovery. It was enough for Anisa to temporarily set aside her friction with Nasser.

"Why didn't you tell me you were discharged?" Hooking a thumb at Nasser, she snapped, "Why didn't he?" She was upset because after he'd vowed that he would report to her the instant Ara had awoken, he'd reneged on his promise.

"Nasser doesn't hold any blame. I told him not to tell you."

Anisa frowned, more confused by all the secrecy. "Why not just tell me?" Then, because she had a sneaking suspicion, she amended sharply, "What aren't you telling me?"

Ara sighed, and somehow that peeved her more.

"I wanted to surprise you, that's all."

Well, he'd succeeded, but now that the joy of seeing him again had passed, it was replaced by a gnawing concern.

"The hospital did clear you to leave, didn't they?" It would be just like Ara to stubbornly check himself out. But he shook his head, allaying her fears that he'd left the professional care he had been receiving earlier than he ought to have.

"The doctor and I decided that I could recuperate at home once my tests came back with positive news."

"That's good," she murmured.

Ara flashed her another smile, the sight of it rejuvenating the warmth that was quelled by her ever-present fears. It didn't last long, because Ara then frowned.

"I heard that an incident occurred in the city center, and that you were almost harmed."

Anisa's jaw dropped, the whiplash switch of emotions confusing her before her head cleared and anger stormed its way to the front. She winged a glare at Nasser and hated how nonchalant he appeared under her baleful stare.

"He told you. Of course he did." She folded her arms.

"Again, Nasser was hired to do his job, Anisa. I asked him to give me reports, and I think it's important. Otherwise I can't protect you properly."

"Protection!" Anisa threw up her hands and laughed mirthlessly, exasperated by these two men and tired of giving them no fight on the final say. "It's all about protection, but neither of you can fully tell me *what* you're protecting me from exactly." She looked between them, their silence backing her point up. They didn't trust her with whatever it was they were up to, and it hurt beyond comprehension. "Well, I'm tired of your protection. I don't want or need it."

Then, without looking back, she stormed out and past her bedroom for the stairs, ignoring Ara calling her name, and pretending her heart wasn't breaking that Nasser seemed to not care whether she stayed or left.

"Is there something happening between you and my sister?"

Nasser ripped his narrowed eyes off the open doors to Ara's study, where he'd only just watched Anisa tear out of the room and had to kill his instinct to follow her. Not only because he sensed that Anisa wasn't happy with him right then, but now Ara was staring at him suspiciously after he posed the question. It was the last thing Nasser expected to happen, and the last subject he wished to discuss.

After nearly getting her killed.

He knew he'd hurt her by his sudden choice to pass her protection over to another, but it had to be done. In her presence, he allowed himself to get distracted, and that had nearly gotten her injured. Or far worse, *killed.*

Some might accuse him of exaggerating, but life was so fragile. Death could come from anywhere. Strike so suddenly that there was no protection from it. That was what had happened to Nuruddin. One second he was holding Nasser's hand and pulling him away from danger, and the next he was crumpling to the ground, dead long before medical aid could arrive.

That could have easily been Anisa a few days earlier. Then she would've died on his watch. Just the notion was enough to break his heart. He wasn't strong enough to protect her—and he didn't believe he'd ever be.

He'd done one final thing for her. Once he'd gotten news of Ara waking from his comatose state, he flew out of Hargeisa to Mogadishu immediately and saw to it personally that Anisa's brother returned home safely to her. He hadn't wanted her to get her hopes up, and so he'd left without saying a word to her, entrusting her safety and care to his reliable staff. Of course, she must have thought he had run away from her.

Rather than battle his fraught emotions, he capped the helplessness rising up in him and confronted Ara's inquiring gaze.

"Between us?" Nasser drawled, affecting nonchalance he didn't feel at all. "Besides professional courtesy, no."

Ara's eyebrows sprang up. "Oh. She seemed awfully upset with you."

Nasser pushed down the guilt that surged at being reminded that he caused any pain to her, and he smoothed his features so as to not reflect anything to confirm Ara's suspicions.

After assessing him for what felt like minutes, Ara nodded briskly. "I had to ask, you know."

"I understand." And he did. If their roles were flipped, he'd want to protect his kid sister too. Anisa might not realize it now, but she had people around her who would do a far better job than he when it came to safeguarding her. These feelings they had for each other would fade with time.

She'll forget me and move on, and it will be for the best.

He wished he could say the same, but as he had no mind to replace her, Nasser was prepared to mourn what he would lose out on when he left her. If only he was a different person…someone who could be enough for her. Needing a focus besides his self-pity, Nasser asked Ara the same thing he'd been asking him the moment he'd awoken from his coma.

"Do you have what I wanted?"

Rolling out from behind his desk to the seating area in his office, Ara motioned for Nasser to take a seat across from him. He didn't speak until Nasser was seated and at eye level with him. "I do. The list is in an encrypted file. Your IT team at my company has the key as they built encryption software for it."

"Forward me the file."

"I already did earlier, on our flight out of Mogadishu," Ara said.

Nasser stood hastily and snapped up his tablet from Ara's desk. He hadn't had time to clear everything off since he'd temporarily taken over his office. It worked to his benefit just then, because within minutes, he had made calls to his team for the decryption code and had access to the very file Ara mentioned.

The names of the culprits who'd had a hand in Nuruddin's death stared him in the face. He'd dreamed of this day for so very long, and now Nasser had a hard time believing what he was looking at. He stopped scrolling, one name in particular having jumped out at him from his tablet's glowing screen.

"Sharmarke." He looked up at Ara, scowling. "Your father-in-law's involved."

"I typed the list, didn't I? I'm aware of what names are on there." Ara sighed, sounding and looking more fatigued by the second. "It's a disappointing revelation at most. I didn't expect it to be true, but I confirmed it. Sharmarke was one of the government officials who sanctioned the attack at the protest rally that killed your brother, Nasser."

He regarded the list again. "Where is he now?"

"Before I tell you, humor me for a moment. Is vengeance still the path you want to walk?"

What kind of question was that? Everything Nasser had done after the day he lost Nuruddin had led him to that moment. Even if he wanted to walk away, he didn't know if any other path was open to him.

That's a lie, and you know it.

Nasser breathed deeply as an image crystallized in his mind. It was of Anisa in his arms, both of them smiling and lost in a happiness of their own making. But just as quickly as he thought of her, he relinquished the futile dream. Being with Anisa was impossible for him. And without her, he had no choice but to fulfill his plot for justice.

Realizing Ara awaited a response, Nasser demanded, "It is. Now tell me where Sharmarke is."

"He's under house arrest currently, while I secure the evidence that will put him away. But if this is the path you're still determined to be on, then go, take your revenge. Either way, it concludes this business of ours."

As Nasser strode out of Ara's study, he recognized that though this *business* with Ara might have ended, that he wasn't quite finished. He had one more stop before he finally sought the revenge he'd wanted.

He only prayed that she didn't turn him out, especially as it could be the last time Nasser saw or spoke to Anisa ever again.

Not long after she marched out of Ara's office in protest at how delicately her brother and Nasser were treating her, a knock on her door had Anisa scrambling out of bed and straightening her hijab. She paused to check her reflection, dashing away the fresh tears streaking down her cheeks and clearing her throat of the sadness that clogged it before she opened her bedroom door.

Nasser stood a respectable distance away, his face as inscrutable as his thoughts and feelings.

"What do you want?" she grumped.

"May I come in?"

"No, because I was just headed out," she snapped, stepping past the threshold and closing the door behind her. The thought of being trapped with him in her bedroom had her heart palpitating wildly. If they were going to have a conversation, she would have the choice of a setting.

She led him down to the kitchen, where she microwaved herself a bowl of buttery popcorn. Grabbing her snack, she then headed for the family room, parked herself in front of the excessively large wall-mounted television, and flipped through movies until she settled on a chilling horror film. Not her usual go-to genre, but her dark mood called for something bloodier. And as terror and chaos played out on the TV and she munched on her popcorn, Anisa could almost pretend every part of her wasn't finely attuned to Nasser's presence so close to her.

Almost.

Because try as she might, she was very aware of him. It irked her, but it was the truth. Rather than calming down, with every passing second Anisa grew more agitated. The movie hadn't even played for a full five minutes when Anisa snatched up the remote, pressed Pause, and lanced Nasser with a glare.

"Are you just going to stand there?" she asked, feeling more waspish now that she was looking at him.

"I'm not staying, Anisa. I only came to tell you that I'm leaving."

She rolled her eyes and scoffed, "Why tell me when you've already left before without saying a word?"

He had the nerve to sigh. "It's because I'm done working with your brother."

"You mean you're done protecting me." She curled her lips into a sneer. It was either that or give in to the tears that began sparking at the corners of her eyes. And she was tired of hiding from these emotions she always seemed to feel around him, needing this off her chest more than anything.

Anisa set her popcorn down on the sofa beside her so it wouldn't impede her from standing, marching right up to him and poking a finger at his face. "It was a heartless move to leave without telling me you were going."

"Heartless?" Nasser's face grew stormier in a blink.

The swift change in him should've been warning enough for her to back off, but she only had a fleeting few seconds of caution before he acted. Faster than she could evade him, he ensnared her wrists and hauled her into him. Though suddenly pressed flush to Nasser, Anisa didn't resist. She was too shocked by his quick actions to process what had happened.

"Is it heartless of me to want to find the people who are responsible for my brother's death? *Punish* them so that they never inflict the damage they did to my family on anyone else?"

He pushed his face closer to hers with every word. By the end of it, he encompassed her whole field of vision.

"No, I'm not heartless to want to seek vengeance on those who hurt me and my family." Their chests were nearly touching now, and his flinty gaze roved lower down her face to where she had drawn her bottom lip between her teeth. She saw a muscle twitch along his jaw, and his brow creased that much more. Now his thumbs stroked tenderly along the sensitive part of her inner wrist. "Not heartless," he murmured, as if he had to convince himself more than her.

And then, just as she seriously thought that he'd kiss her—

He let her go abruptly.

Gawking at him, Anisa touched her wrists and swayed in place at the sudden loss of his touch.

Nasser raked a hand over his short black curls, his palm snapping around the back of his neck. He rolled his shoulders, a strained look crossing his face. "The reason I'm leaving is that your brother promised me something in exchange for your protection. I wanted the names of the people who'd had a hand in killing my brother. Not the men who pulled the trigger, but those that hid behind their bureaucratic titles and public offices.

"When Nuruddin was killed, *I* was accused of his death. Do you know what it's like to be labeled a criminal and a monster and be locked up falsely? To be a scapegoat for the politicians who killed my brother? Then to be forced into the military by those same politicians who only hoped that I would be killed in the line of duty somewhere and make their lives easier?"

He stared at her with hellfire in his eyes. "I didn't die though. And now I want what I've always wanted since my brother was murdered. I want vengeance. Justice. I want to right wrongs, and I intend to do so." Then, seeing his head turn toward the exit from the family room, Anisa rushed around him and blocked his escape.

She stopped shy of throwing out her arms dramatically, instead trying to use her words to calm him. "There has to be another way." Anisa gazed at him pleadingly and clung to the hope that she could dissuade him from leaving on some violent mission to avenge his late brother.

"Anisa, you can't stop me."

She knew that she couldn't.

But I can try.

"So, what do you plan to do when you find these responsible parties?"

Nasser gave her a look that chilled her blood. From that one glance, she inferred that he meant to take his ultimate revenge.

Panicked, Anisa breached his space, pushed up on her toes and got up in his face.

"You can't do what you're thinking, Nasser. It won't bring Nuruddin back. And I'm certain he wouldn't want you killing yourself with all this guilt. Because your brother's death isn't your fault."

"*Because* of me, my parents had to bury their son prematurely. *My* mistake killed my brother. *Mine.*"

"Is that how you feel, Nasser, or is that what your parents told you?" And when he didn't respond, Anisa kept on, her hope that she was getting through to him cemented when his brows furrowed with consideration. "Maybe they feel different than you do. Maybe they never blamed you, and all they want is for you to be happy and free of this burden of responsibility for your brother's passing."

The longer Nasser remained quiet, the more hopeful she was that she'd saved him from making a life-altering mistake.

But she came crashing down to reality when he cleared his face of any emotion, locking her out of his thoughts and feelings.

"And what if your parents' death wasn't an accident? What if you knew the names of the people who killed them?"

Anisa reared back from him as though he had dealt her a physical blow. His cruel words certainly packed the same punch, leaving her ridden with senselessness. And when she finally did feel something, it was abject disappointment in him for stooping so low and using her parents' deaths to make a point about why he had to fulfill his revenge plot.

A part of her knew that he was doing this on purpose to force her into pushing him away.

But she was too tired to call him out on it. So she didn't. "I can't stop you, can I?" she said sadly.

"You're better off letting me go," he replied.

Tightening her lips to keep herself from sobbing, Anisa moved aside and watched helplessly as Nasser breezed past her.

Since meeting him, she'd always accepted that they'd eventually go their separate ways. But she hadn't realized until that instant just how difficult it would be to allow him to walk away from her again. Anisa wanted to be enraged with him, yet all she felt was heartache. For him. For his brother. For his family.

For us.

Or what they could have been had Nasser not chosen his revenge over her.

CHAPTER TWELVE

SINCE LEAVING BERBERA nearly a week ago, Nasser didn't feel as strongly motivated by his mission of vengeance.

It started when he'd followed the address Ara had given him to the remote home that imprisoned Sharmarke. Nasser sat across from the evil man and stared him in the eye with the knowledge that he'd played a role in delivering Nuruddin to an early grave and then sending Nasser to prison along with other innocent protestors. He imagined throttling him many times, reaching over the table that separated them and choking him before the guards Ara had stationed outside the plain one-room house heard the mischief and caught on to what was taking place right under their noses.

But the more he looked at the old, tired man sitting hunched and in a rumpled suit across from him, the less anger he felt. If anything, he pitied him for the poor choices he'd made, and seeing the hopelessness in his eyes was as satisfying as watching the life go out of him at his hands. Nasser left him alive and as well as anyone could be while housebound and with the only freedom they could look forward to being the prison that awaited them.

Not even bothering to pursue the other names on the list Ara gave him, he'd then flown straight to Hargeisa, where his parents lived after having moved from Djibouti a long time ago, and where he had grown up along with Nuruddin. He'd dropped in and surprised them. His mother nearly collapsed from joy, and even his stoic father had smiled tearfully and hugged him for longer than usual. It had been a long time since he'd visited, worried every time he did that the love they had for him would change to hatred and blame. He wouldn't fault them if they did resent him.

Now, after a few days spent in the comfort of his family, he traveled to the place he had visited only once before.

He stood over his brother's grave and the stone covering the hole that was Nuruddin's final resting place. Nasser crouched and traced the etching in the stone, spelling out Nuruddin's full name and his birthdate and death date. The only other time he'd been here was right after he had been freed from prison and forced to sign up for military service. And he'd only come because his parents compelled him to; he hadn't wanted to confront his guilt immediately.

So he imagined it had come as a shock to them when he'd asked to visit Nuruddin.

Standing behind him now, his parents watched as Nasser pressed his palm in the center of the sun-warmed stone.

"I missed the chance to see him properly buried." He stood and looked back at his parents, his heart aching. "I suppose it's divine punishment." Unable to hold their gazes for this next part, he cast his burning eyes down to Nuruddin's grave and said what he hadn't been able to tell them for all these years. "It's my fault he died."

His mother gasped, the sound followed by her hurrying over to him and taking his face into her hands. "Look at me, Nasser. You are not responsible for what happened."

"We don't blame you. How could we when you're all we have left?" His father came up to them, his hand gripping and squeezing Nasser's shoulder.

Kissing his cheeks, his mother took his hands and pressed them to her chest. "You're our pride and joy. We miss Nuruddin, of course, but it doesn't diminish what we feel for you. We'll always love you, Nasser, and we'll always love your brother, too."

Blinking back tears, Nasser hung his head, taking in their words and recognizing the peace that came with them. For so long he'd bottled what he had been feeling for fear and shame that he'd only bring more pain to his parents. He'd even kept the truth of Nuruddin's death from them to spare them.

But now, as they held him and reaffirmed their love for him, Nasser fought past the lump in his throat and told them everything.

About how Nuruddin tried to save him. And how he'd been gunned down right in front of Nasser.

The crooked government officials who'd been behind Nuruddin's death had spun the media coverage of the violent use of force at the rally as having been necessary. They painted the peaceful protestors as rebels. They had then told Nasser's parents that they should be grateful their son had only been forcefully conscripted into the military.

It all came tumbling out of him. When the full truth was aired, he sighed long and hard, an oppressive weight he hadn't recognized shifting off him.

His parents shared a look when he finished speaking. Then his father nodded solemnly. "We know." And before Nasser could ask how, his mother explained.

"We heard from the others who escaped the protest." She named a friend of Nuruddin's and then said, "He came to visit us about a year after you'd left to board at the military academy, and he told us everything about that awful day. About what you and Nuruddin both suffered."

"Why didn't you tell me that you knew?" Nasser asked once his shock passed.

"It was a decision your mother and I made. We didn't see a reason to open up an old wound. What happened to your brother..." his father trailed off, blinking suspiciously "...was terrible. But we still had you, and we only wished to do right by you."

They wanted to spare *his* feelings. Nasser couldn't believe what he was hearing, considering he'd invested all this energy trying to protect them from the truth of Nuruddin's death.

When in reality they've been doing the exact same thing for me.

Suddenly an urge to laugh struck him hard, so he did.

He threw his head back from the laughter. Wiping at his eyes as his humor wound down, he noticed his parents traded worried looks.

"I'm fine," he reassured them. "I only just remembered something funny."

He chuckled again at how silly he'd been all these years. Not once had he even thought that his parents would want to protect him too, in their own way. Now that he knew better, Nasser stared at them through new eyes.

"Thank you." He embraced them both, smiling down at them. "I'm sorry that I haven't been around very much, but that'll change now. I promise you."

As they bade Nuruddin farewell and walked

down the dusty hill to where Nasser had parked his truck, his mother leaned into him and said, "Although we love seeing you, your father and I were surprised by your sudden visit."

His father interjected then, "I thought you said we weren't going to ask him."

His mother flapped a hand dismissively. "I changed my mind," she said, to which his father clucked his tongue.

Nasser smiled at their lighthearted banter, wondering how he could have ever allowed his misplaced guilt to get him to stay away from them.

"We just want to know if anything's wrong, Nasser," his mother told him. "Anything that might have brought you home to us."

"Nothing's wrong," he replied. As to why he'd come for a visit, Nasser thought of Anisa. She had planted the seed for him to go see his parents—for him to open up about his feelings to them. If he had anyone to thank for this peaceful bubble he was wrapped up in now, it was her.

But he couldn't see her.

Not after the way he'd ended things.

"A friend advised that I should visit you."

"Oh? We'll have to thank this friend of yours one day then," his mother said with a loving pat to his arm.

Then, instead of waxing poetic about how Anisa was amusingly stubborn, beautiful, creative, and easy to talk to, he regaled them with the adventures he'd shared with her. From the lemur who decided to do its business on his shoulder, to the handline fishing they'd done on the beach together. Though they were memories he would treasure forever, Nasser didn't want them to remain as only memories.

He certainly didn't want those memories to be the only pieces he had of her.

I love her, he thought, so very naturally.

He loved her and he'd messed up what might have become a really good thing with her. And all for what? Because he'd believed that he couldn't protect her. Nasser scoffed inwardly, surprised that he hadn't seen she never needed his protection—at least not in the way he imagined. And that just like his parents had tried to protect him, Anisa had done so in her own way. She'd attempted to shield him from seeking out the revenge that would ultimately have only ended up hurting him. Somehow she had known that his vengeance wouldn't give him the pleasure he once believed it might.

Nasser shook his head, disgusted with himself.

But he stopped there, not beating himself up about it any longer, his mind already spinning as he thought of what he could do to win her back.

Nasser leaving again shouldn't have been new to Anisa, but it felt different the second time.

Because I know he's not coming back.

He'd said so himself before he left her. Before he had gone off to chase after his so-called idea of justice for his brother.

She wasn't important enough to him, obviously. And yet here she was, giving him way more thought than he deserved.

Deciding that staying busy would get her to move forward, Anisa turned back to her writing. She'd also extended her stay in Berbera, not yet ready to leave Ara, even though she was still upset with him for crossing a line and trying to exert his control over her. Ara was the reason that Nasser came into her life, after all. Her brother was partly to blame for this heartbreak she was nursing. The other part was solely on her. Even before learning that Nasser had only protected her to get information from Ara for his mission of revenge, she'd known deep down that Nasser was the last man she should fall in love with.

Because it was love.

Still young and new, but powerful enough to leave her staring off into space while quietly fretting for his safety.

What if he does something stupid and gets himself hurt?

She'd already had to handle Ara just being out of the woods. Anisa couldn't bear the thought of another person she cared about getting hurt.

As the days passed, her anxiety only doubled down and injected its poison into her dreams. The nightmares she'd once had of being run over by speeding motorboats and drowning along with her parents had turned into terror for Nasser's well-being. She started sleeping less and less, avoiding her bed for fear that her bad dreams would somehow be self-fulfilling.

In an effort to keep from falling asleep, she alternated between writing, watching films and TV shows, and pacing the halls at night. She might have walked the grounds outside and stretched her legs had she not figured the guards would report to Ara about her night wanderings. The last thing she wanted was to give him a reason to hover over her more.

And since she couldn't go outside as easily as she would have liked, Anisa settled for getting some fresh air up on the rooftop terrace.

She hadn't gone up there until Nasser had left, not having a reason to explore before then. But now that she had, she could see why Ara had paid for it to be built when he'd remodeled their childhood home. It was beautiful up there, the spacious seating area around a firepit and the touches of greenery seamlessly melding beauty with comfort and luxury.

Once she discovered how peaceful it was, Anisa began going up to the terrace to calm herself.

That night was no different.

She hoped for a quiet moment to herself. Instead, she came to a fast stop when she saw that she wasn't alone.

Ara stood a few feet from her, his wheelchair nowhere in sight but a cane within arm's reach. The only reason he hadn't noticed her was that he had his back to her and his hand raised, his cell phone pressed to his ear. It was hard to tell who he was talking to as she could barely catch what he said in his deep, murmuring tone. The words she did hear didn't make sense.

"Let's talk later…No, not now…This isn't the time…"

Though she couldn't hear the other side of the conversation, Anisa gleaned from Ara's tense posturing that it wasn't a chat he was happy to be having.

She was only now recalling that Nasser had told her Ara liked the terrace most. Apparently even being wheelchair-bound in his condition wasn't enough to stop her brother from coming upstairs. And now his cane made perfect sense since a stairway connected the terrace to the house's lower floors.

Silently cursing herself for forgetting, she immediately started backing away from him. As curious as she was about who the caller was and what the call was about that had Ara sounding so flustered, Anisa didn't think he'd appreciate her listening in on him. Before she could tiptoe away without him ever knowing she'd been there, Ara suddenly pulled the phone down from his ear and turned, his eyes landing on her.

"Anisa," he said, sounding as surprised as he appeared. Then he frowned. "What are you doing up here so late?"

She resisted poking her tongue out at him, her humiliation at looking like she'd been eavesdropping disappearing in a puff of smoke and replaced by her annoyance.

"I could ask you the same question." She crossed her arms.

He shook his head. "As I'm sure you just heard, I was taking a phone call."

She narrowed her eyes. "I barely heard anything. And if I had known you were up here, I wouldn't have disturbed you."

"Did I accuse you of disturbing me?"

Anisa harrumphed, not knowing why he'd reduced her to feeling like a little kid again with one lightly scolding remark. How was it that after four years of being her own person, and of not having to rely on Ara, she hadn't shed this keen need for his approval?

It heaped more irritation onto her already sour mood. And since she didn't think she had anything nice to say, she turned away and only stopped at the sound of her name.

"Anisa, wait." The sound of Ara's cane tap-tap-tapping on the terrace's stone flooring came up behind her. "We should have a talk, shouldn't we? A proper one. It's been years, after all."

Her arms still folded, she faced him and nodded quickly, knowing that this day would have eventually come. The fact that they hadn't spoken for so very long was the elephant in the room.

"There's something I've been meaning to say. Something I should have said the moment I saw you again." He took a deep breath and then said, "I'm sorry, Anisa."

Anisa blinked fast, at first certain she hadn't heard him correctly, and then feeling tears forming already when Ara had barely spoken.

"I apologize for not having ended our silence earlier. It was childish of me. No, it was downright *wrong*. When I awoke in the hospital, I thought of you first." Ara's lips twitched up, a small smile wiping the signs of strain from his features.

It had to be taking much of his effort to stand upright when he still wasn't feeling all that well. Knowing that he was pushing through his discomfort for her had Anisa's bottom lip trembling and her heart throbbing with compassion. She would've opened her mouth to stop him so he could rest, but Ara jutted his chin upwards in determination, propped both hands over his cane and held himself as tall as he could in his still-recovering state.

"I thought that I wouldn't see you again, and it put these past years without you in my life into perspective. Anisa, I don't expect your forgiveness, but I'm asking—no, *hoping* that you'll let me earn your trust back as your brother. Please."

She wiped at her eyes at his proposal, sniffled loudly and laughed. "Great. You've made me cry."

Ara laughed with her. And just like that, the tension between them evaporated.

Still wiping at her eyes, Anisa said, "I'm sorry, too. I could have picked up the phone and given you a call. I was too stubborn."

"Must be a family trait," he teased. Then he eased back on his cane and gestured for her to join him on the terrace. Standing at the very edge of the rooftop deck and looking out over their home city, Ara told her, "I'm glad you're home. It doesn't feel as lonely with you here."

"Lonely? You shouldn't let your wife hear you say that. Speaking of, where is she, and when do I get to meet her finally? Her name's Zaynab, right?" It was really all Anisa knew of his wife. Besides that she was raised by her mother primarily in the UK after her parents divorced. Sharmarke had remarried a long time ago, and he hadn't spoken of Zaynab, not until he'd messaged Anisa with the news that Ara had married his daughter and they had become real family through marriage.

"I still can't believe you're married," she remarked, snorting then. "I hope she knew what she was getting into."

"We're actually getting divorced."

Anisa goggled at him. "Divorced? Why?"

"It's complicated, but you might as well know." Then he told her Adeero Sharmarke was involved in the deadly assault at the protest that killed Nasser's brother, Nuruddin.

Anisa dropped onto one of the cushioned benches nearby, shocked to her core by this turn of events. "I can't believe Adeero Sharmarke would do that."

Ara's sigh was long-suffering. It made her wonder how long he'd kept this information to himself. She knew it had to be a while judging by the way he sounded more fatigued than he had seconds earlier.

"Ten months ago, I reached out to Nasser because I liked what I was hearing about his company's security services. We got to talking, and I learned he lost his brother at a protest rally in Hargeisa years ago. I knew that Sharmarke worked in government around that time in the city, but whenever I tried broaching the subject with him, he would casually dismiss me.

"That was my first red flag. So, I did the research without Sharmarke's help. And what you're feeling was how I felt when I first started looking into the protest for Nasser. The more I dug into the government files I could get my hands on, the more I noticed Sharmarke's name alongside other crooked politicians, and the more I'd hoped it wasn't true—that there was some mistake somewhere, and he wasn't involved. But he was one of several who had signed off on the use of deadly force at the protest. Though he hadn't killed Nasser's brother outright himself, he might as well have."

His brows furrowed in consternation. "I had a choice then. Conceal the truth...or try and accept that Adeero Sharmarke wasn't who we believed him to be. I chose acceptance, and part of that meant telling Nasser the truth."

As soon as the words were out of his mouth, Anisa sucked in a sharp inhale, and her spine went ramrod-straight. "*That's* why Nasser left. You let him go after Sharmarke. What if he gets hurt?"

What if he dies?

Ara sat down beside her, a look of relief briefly streaking over his face as he stretched his legs out and set his cane aside.

"Given what he does for a living, I feel confident that Nasser can protect himself," Ara said, but taking her hand and rubbing her knuckles in comfort when her worry for Nasser didn't fade. "It's Sharmarke I'm more concerned about, but I've stationed men to keep Nasser from doing too much damage."

"Ara," Anisa whispered, her whole face itching with the urge to cry anew.

"As much as Sharmarke might deserve it, I

won't let Nasser make the mistake of killing a man and tainting his soul."

Full of gratitude, but unable to put it into words around the big lump in her throat, she curled into Ara's side. He wrapped his arm around her shoulders, embracing her as best as he could with his healing wounds. It reminded her of when she was younger, after their parents died, and Anisa would wake from one of her night terrors. Never too far away, Ara would show up and comfort her until the terrifying feeling of loneliness vanished. Until she remembered that she wasn't ever alone, not so long as she and Ara had each other.

Anisa thought they were finished with all the soul-baring, but when she peeled back from Ara to wipe her eyes, she froze at the troubling frown on his face.

"There's something else. It regards *Hooyo* and *Aabo*."

She pushed up onto her feet, suddenly feeling like she needed to go for the longest run of her life—but she settled for pacing in front of Ara and feeling his eyes follow her carefully.

"What about them?" she asked, wringing her hands.

"It's about how they died."

For the next several minutes, Ara turned her world upside down. He told her that their parents hadn't died in an accident but were murdered in cold blood. Anisa sobbed through most of it, horrified that someone had torn their family apart purposefully. And that she'd nearly died along with their parents. By the end, Anisa scrubbed at her face, her eyes feeling raw.

She now understood why Ara had tried to protect her all this time. Why he'd made their home one big fortress. Why he'd sent Nasser to her. He wanted to safeguard her from the monsters who had killed their mom and dad.

"I wish you'd told me earlier," she said. "It hurts even more knowing that you suffered by yourself, and I couldn't protect you like you protected me." Anisa hugged him then, squeezing Ara tightly. "Thank you. For thinking of me, putting me before you, and just being my family."

When she began to let him go, Anisa felt Ara's arms tightening around her, quietly indicating he didn't want to release her just yet.

"Anisa, you just being with me now is enough to protect me from feeling like I'll drown in my sorrow." He slowly released her then, smiling at her, his eyes dark with unshed tears.

"Did they find who...?" Anisa couldn't bear to say *killed our parents*, but thankfully Ara understood her and answered with a slow, sad shake of his head.

"That's why I've been working with Nasser. After I learned of what had happened to his brother, I thought perhaps the same culprits were behind our parents' deaths."

"You thought Sharmarke did it?"

"I was wrong there, and I would say *thankfully*, but considering what he did to Nasser and his family, I don't think it would be appropriate."

Anisa nodded in agreement, her mind trailing now that Nasser had been mentioned. After everything Ara had revealed to her, it wasn't surprising that she'd been too preoccupied to think of anything or *anyone* else. But now Nasser was all she could think of again. And the subject of how her parents died reminded her of what Nasser had said to her in their last conversation a few days ago.

She'd thought Nasser's insinuation that her parents were killed was unusually cruel. Now she knew that he had only tried to warn her of the truth. Like Ara, Nasser had just been trying to protect her. And like Ara, all she'd done was push him away in fear that his secrets would cause friction between them. That because he was choosing to hide a part of himself away. He didn't trust her. So how could he care for her?

The truth was, she was still scared he could harm her. More so because Anisa knew she loved him.

But he hadn't hurt her thus far, and that had to count for something. At the very least, to spare herself from future regret, Anisa felt compelled to tell him the truth about her feelings for him.

She had all these wasted years of time lost with

Ara to mourn. She wouldn't do the same thing with Nasser.

"I have to go," she suddenly announced, hugging her brother before bouncing up to her feet.

Ara gave her a confused look but said nothing and didn't stop her from hurrying away from him.

Anisa raced back to her bedroom, an idea forming in her mind. She rummaged through her luggage and pulled out Nasser's business card. He'd once told her that she could call the number on the card to verify his credentials. Now it might be the only way to get to him. It was perhaps pointless to try, but she wanted to, knowing that this was her last shot at making things right.

Her last chance at bringing Nasser back to her.

My last hope that he'll choose me.

CHAPTER THIRTEEN

WHEN NASSER RECEIVED a call from his main office and discovered from his executive secretary that Anisa had called and left a vague message asking to speak to him as soon as possible, he didn't know what to think except that the universe clearly wanted them to be together.

Not wanting to fumble it with her this time, he dropped everything overnight to drive out to Berbera from his parents' home in Hargeisa.

His mother and father weren't too happy with him for leaving, but they settled down once Nasser promised that he'd return.

"An important meeting came up, and I can't reschedule it," he had fibbed. He didn't want to let his parents in on anything if nothing would come of it. For all Nasser knew, she'd called for something mundane.

That was why he was going to see her.

If she was planning to shatter his heart, he wanted it to be in person. At least that way he could see her one last time.

It was fairly late at night when he'd left Hargeisa and even later by the time his truck's headlights beamed brightly on the steel gates to Anisa and Ara's family home.

The guards cleared him to pass through.

Ara was waiting for him in the foyer, sitting tall and confident in his wheelchair, his neutral expression not giving away how he felt about Nasser visiting so late and without forewarning.

"I didn't know we had an appointment," he said.

Nasser's mouth went dry. He'd been in such a rush to see Anisa that he hadn't given much thought to what to say to her overprotective older brother.

"We don't have an appointment." And before he was forced to think up a lie on the spot, a familiar voice he longed to hear came floating down from above them.

"I called him."

Nasser's heart gave a jolt as his head snapped up. Anisa came bounding down the stairs in fuzzy slippers, her oversized knit sweater and black loose-fit jeans giving her a homey look. She had her glasses on again, her eyes wide behind the hexagonal frames.

"You're here to see my sister."

"I am," Nasser said, his mouth drying because he had a hard time peeling his gaze off Anisa, and because Ara's hawkish stare seemed to assess him for any danger he might pose Anisa.

Still looking at Nasser unblinkingly, Ara asked Anisa, "Can we talk?"

They walked a little way from where he stood before speaking, and Ara, not seeming to care whether Nasser heard him or not, spoke loudly.

"Say the word and I'll send him away."

Nasser tensed at Ara's threat, his hands clenching into fists as he fought the urge to adjust his collar and relieve the heat slashing over the back of his neck.

The only thing that relaxed him was Anisa's laugh.

It has to be a good sign that she's in a humorous mood.

"Remember, I told you I called him," she said once her laughter subsided. "It would be rude if you sent him away."

"Are you sure?" he intoned.

Nasser was in awe that Anisa didn't wilt before Ara's drilling gaze.

She shook her head. "I know you're only trying to protect me." Then, leaning down, she kissed Ara's cheek, hugged her brother, and pulled back from him. "I've got this though. I love you, but I promise I can protect myself too."

Ara's mouth opened, but whatever he said was too soft for Nasser to hear.

If he had to guess, he would say that Ara told

Anisa he loved her too. It certainly would explain why Anisa came walking over to him with a smile full of her inner joy. Looking at her beautiful smiling face, he was struck by the instinct to take her into his arms and kiss her. And Nasser might have given in to the temptation if he hadn't noticed Ara watching them.

Returning his sharp look, Nasser tried to communicate that he wasn't here to harm Ara's sister, and that he wouldn't ever do anything to hurt her.

Not again.

After what felt like a long while, Ara bobbed his head once at Nasser and wheeled back. It seemed he'd been cleared to speak to Anisa. Still, even though Ara rolled away into another room and left them alone in the entrance hall, Nasser couldn't help but feel that he was being watched and tested.

One wrong move and I'm certain he'll drive me out.

Not only out of their home, but out of Anisa's life.

He didn't even care that he'd lose Ara's business. All he cared about in that moment was undoing the damage he'd caused to her impression of him.

"Do you want to go for a walk on the beach?" she asked.

"Yes," Nasser said quickly, feeling like he'd

be able to talk more freely out of earshot of her brother.

Less than half an hour later, they were exiting his truck and navigating their way toward the dark waters of the ocean.

Anisa took off her sandals, dangling them from her hands as they fell into step.

Following suit, Nasser slipped off his socks and Italian leather shoes, once again realizing he hadn't really dressed for their beach outing. But it only reminded him of how quickly he'd hurried to answer her summons. And how *desperately* he didn't want to ruin this opportunity she'd given him to fix the mistake he'd made with her.

He was admittedly nervous, but he wasn't going to squander this moment. Fortifying himself, he said, "My secretary informed me that you called. I only received the message a couple hours ago." Then, wanting to address how cold and insensitive he'd been the last time he saw her, Nasser blurted, "Truthfully? I didn't think I'd hear from you again."

"Are you upset that I called?"

Nasser couldn't help himself when she asked that. He reached out instinctively, taking her arm and gently drawing her to a standstill with him. Now facing each other, the light of a crescent moon barely casting shadows on the beach, he looked down into her eyes and unstuck his tongue from the roof of his mouth.

"Upset? How could I be upset when I wanted to see you?"

"Why?"

He breathed more shallowly, a pressure manifesting over his chest, right above his heart. "I didn't like what I said to you last time. It's haunted me since I left you. Because you were right. Vengeance wasn't the answer." He bared his soul, telling Anisa about the emptiness he'd felt upon facing one of his brother's killers, Sharmarke, and the warmth of being honest with his parents about Nuruddin. He needed her to know that he trusted her with everything. Every part of him could now be hers if she wanted it.

So it was worrying that she moved back from him, forcing his hand to fall off her arm.

She then hugged herself and stared at him, her eyes owlish behind her glasses and full of wariness.

He didn't blame her for being leery of him after he'd gone from hot to cold and back in a span of days. Only now he knew that the feverish heat she'd inspired in him would never let him go— and he didn't want it to.

Not ever.

"Anisa," he said, holding his ground and giving her the space she clearly needed. "I would have come back even if you hadn't left the message. I was planning how I would do it." He had gone through several scenarios, from finding an excuse to have a meeting with Ara at his house to staging an encounter with her while pretending to do updates to Ara's home security features. "I was beginning to run out of plausible ideas to get a chance to speak with you, and then your message came through. I knew our meeting again was fated."

Anisa hugged her arms tighter before finally whispering, "I want to believe you. I do..."

"But you can't," he finished for her.

She sighed. "It's just that I don't want to hope and get hurt again."

Nasser was stricken by her words. All his effort to protect her hadn't taken into account that he'd been the reason she was hurting so badly right now.

Maybe that was why he skipped everything he'd planned to tell her and leaped to the crux of why he had driven at ungodly speeds to close the distance between them and see her again. "I love you."

When she stared at him, her eyes doubling in size and her lips parting in awe, Nasser repeated it for her.

"I'm in love with you, Anisa, and that's why I'm here."

He loved her?

Anisa wouldn't have trusted her own ears if she didn't see for herself that his eyes shone with the proof. He looked at her as though she was all that mattered. Not his vengeance or his secrets or his driving need to protect her. Just her.

"I know that I've hurt you, but if it's any reassurance, I hurt myself even more," he continued, uncharacteristically breathless. From the moment she came down the stairs and rescued him from Ara's interrogation, Anisa had sensed a change in him. And she could hear it for herself and see it in the way Nasser's chest rose and fell quickly. His words rushed out of him like he couldn't speak fast enough to capture all that he felt.

Naturally Anisa's qualms slowly and surely vanished, one by one, leaving her with a restlessness to go to him.

But she held back, knowing that if she went to him right then, she wouldn't be able to say what was on her mind. Following his sweet confession of love for her, it was the hardest thing to stand apart from him, and he only made it more difficult when his face darkened with heartbreaking disappointment.

"The reason I called you, Nasser, was because I didn't like how we ended things either. I shouldn't have let you walk away, even if at the time I thought that was what you needed." She gulped, nervousness pricking at her. "It was the same with Ara. I pushed him away because I believed it was what he wanted, and I was wrong. It was like you told me. He didn't call or message me for all that time because he was scared that I'd reject him."

"You two mended things then," Nasser said with a nod and smile. "Good."

"I'm glad that you and your parents managed to talk, too." She could see that speaking to his family had been good for him. The haunted look in his eyes the last time she saw him was gone. "I guess we both learned that we should be honest about our feelings with those we love."

"And what about us? Where do we stand now?" he asked softly.

Nasser had given her everything she had once asked of him. The sheer honesty and openness, and above all else the complete trust in her. Anisa didn't need to think about it, quietly inching forward then, her bare feet gliding over the sand to him, her toes digging in when she stood before him with very little space between them.

"I think," she began, her heart thumping in her ears, "that we're far better than before."

Nasser responded by taking the hand she wasn't holding her sandals with and running his thumb over her knuckles.

Anisa leaned into him then, her cheek pressing into his chest, and feeling his chin settle over her head. He let go of her hand and embraced her. The cozy warmth suffusing her heart and spreading out from her core changed into a fiery need in the blink of an eye. Gripping the front of his shirt and turning her blushing face up to him, she said, "I also think that we can stand a whole lot closer."

His deep, throaty laugh thrummed through her, his mirth becoming her own.

"Odd," he said then, his face closing in on hers. Their lips brushed softly as he murmured against her mouth, "I was thinking the exact same thing."

Anisa didn't know if it was her long anticipation or the relief that he loved her that weakened her legs more. Thankfully, Nasser stabilized her and allowed Anisa to deepen their kiss. He returned her passion with just as much enthusiasm. When they came up for air, she gasped, "I love you," her face flushing with the embarrassing realization that she hadn't told him before.

But with twinkling eyes, Nasser merely said, "I know, Anisa. I know."

EPILOGUE

A year later

ANISA WAGGLED HER fingers at Darya and their
other friends, smiling widely at their apprecia-
tive noises when the sunlight sparkled off her
new and now most treasured piece of jewelry.
The engagement ring was not the first beautiful
gift Nasser had given her, and frankly, it wasn't
even her favorite.

No, that was reserved for the cheap but pretty
phone chain Nasser had given to her a year ago,
shortly after he'd declared his love to her and she
had returned his feelings. The chain had replaced
the one she'd broken when they first met. Nasser
had bought it while they'd been in Nosy Be for
the jazz festival—he just hadn't told her.

Still, as much as she adored the phone chain,
she couldn't stop staring at or touching the engagement ring. Even now, she found herself stroking the diamond lovingly, to the amusement of
Darya, who nudged her with a grin.

"So, tell me, are you more in love with the gorgeous ring or the equally gorgeous man?"

Anisa looked up, her eyes easily finding Nasser in the crowd of their friends and family. He was looking at her, too, somehow holding a conversation with her brother and sharing a secret smile with her from afar.

"The man. Definitely the man," Anisa said to Darya.

How was it that she fell more in love with him with each passing day? And she knew Nasser felt the same about her, constantly letting her in on how grouchy he became when work pulled him away from her—or her work kept them apart for some time. It happened more now that she'd quit her job as a production assistant, moved back to Berbera permanently, finished her script, secured a film agent, and successfully pitched her idea to a small but growing production company. Anisa still had a way to go before she saw her creativity come to life on-screen, but she was several steps closer, and just happy that she was finally doing what she always wanted to do for a career.

Nasser was busy, too, expanding his business and extending his services to those who might not have the money and means to afford what his wealthier clientele could access. He even began recruiting young men who had left the military in Somaliland and were looking for a good job to provide for their families. It meant that he was looking into opening an office in Hargeisa, nearer to her and the life they wanted to build together.

Now that they had a wedding to plan, Anisa was all the happier that he'd gone down the path that he had with his career.

In that way, they had that much more to celebrate than just announcing their engagement to all their loved ones.

Anisa cast him another look and saw him gesture to her to follow him. He excused himself from Ara and the other people he was speaking to and walked away.

She trailed after him, muffling a yelp when his hand shot out from around a quiet corner and drew her into his hard chest.

He tipped her chin up and gave her a sweet, toe-curling peck on the mouth.

"Stop," she chided, lightly swatting him and looking around for any eyes on them. "What will my brother, your parents and all our other guests think if they catch us?"

"That we should skip this engagement and turn the congratulatory party into a wedding."

She poked at his chest gently. "Don't tease me like that—I'm already stressing about planning a wedding in a year. The thought of doing it in one day…" She mockingly shuddered at his implied deadline, biting back a soft moan when his hands framed her hips and pulled her harder into him. "Keep that up and you'll have us married this second if my brother and your parents have their way. Anything to prevent a scandal."

"I'm bargaining on it," he said with a smug smile before he stole another kiss from her.

He finally let her go when their names were called. Before the search party discovered them and set off gossiping tongues about premarital escapades, Nasser offered her his elbow like a gentleman and guided her back to their guests. They did the rounds, greeting and thanking everyone. Anisa had worried most about Nasser's parents, but his mother and father were more than welcoming. Pleased by the news their son was getting married, they'd practically adopted her the instant he'd introduced them. She'd gained a form of surrogate parents in them.

"I hope my mother and father aren't being too pushy," Nasser said to her when he had her alone next, only this time it was out in the open so that neither of them would be as easily tempted to sneak kisses and prolonged touches.

"Pushy?" Anisa wrinkled her nose and shook her head immediately. "No way! I think they had a good idea about potentially looking into a guest space for them once we're married and moved into our new home."

"Let's table that. I'm not ready to share you just yet." Nasser's laughter rumbled through her as he pulled her closer against him. When she tried to push him away, he only held her tighter, breathing into her ear, "Don't worry. No one's looking, so let me hold you a little longer."

After that she didn't have the heart to try to wriggle free, not that she ever really wanted to in the first place.

When Anisa did finally pull back enough to look around, she realized with a start that some-one was missing. "Where's Ara?"

Darya was within earshot, and she turned to them and pointed toward the exit. "I just saw your brother walk out. There was a woman with him." She went on to describe the woman. Nasser told Anisa, "That sounds like Zaynab. His wife."

"Soon to be ex-wife," Anisa reminded him, keeping her voice low so as to not generate a rumor. Ara was already dealing with the final-ization of his divorce. Zaynab seemed like a nice person, but Anisa didn't know what to think of her in light of the impending marital dissolution. All she'd seen was Ara's quiet torment. She wasn't sure if it was because he felt like he owed Zaynab something after her father, Sharmarke, was of-ficially sentenced to prison for the cover-up of Nasser's brother Nuruddin's death and other po-litical corruption schemes, or if Ara truly cared about her.

"Should we go after him?" she asked Nasser.

He frowned, shaking his head slowly. "We could, but he's an adult, Anisa. If he wanted our help, I'm sure he would have asked us."

She knew Nasser was right. It was just that she felt as though Ara could use her help for once.

Reading her mind, Nasser gave her a hug. She melted into his arms, blushing when she caught the stares of some of their guests who had noticed their lengthy embrace.

"Nasser, everyone's beginning to look at us," she remarked, trying to pull back, only to feel his arms cage around her tighter.

"Let them stare. All they're seeing anyways is a man who is hopelessly and perpetually smitten with his lovely new fiancée."

Anisa smiled brightly, seeing his logic for herself. Then, closing her eyes, she held him to her heart, where Nasser was and always would be, and where she knew without a doubt that he held her too.

* * * * *

*If you enjoyed this story,
check out these other great reads from
Hana Sheik:*

The Baby Swap That Bound Them
Forbidden Kisses with Her Millionaire Boss
Temptation in Istanbul

All available now!